Leah vs. Art

ALSO BY JOY McCULLOUGH &
VEEDA BYBEE

Jojo vs. Middle School

JOY McCULLOUGH & VEEDA BYBEE

Team Awkward #2
Leah vs. Art

ALADDIN NEW YORK   AMSTERDAM/ANTWERP   LONDON
TORONTO   SYDNEY/MELBOURNE   NEW DELHI

This book is a work of fiction. Any references to historical events, real people, or real places are used fictitiously. Other names, characters, places, and events are products of the author's imagination, and any resemblance to actual events or places or persons, living or dead, is entirely coincidental.

ALADDIN

An imprint of Simon & Schuster Children's Publishing Division
1230 Avenue of the Americas, New York, New York 10020
For more than 100 years, Simon & Schuster has championed authors and the stories they create. By respecting the copyright of an author's intellectual property, you enable Simon & Schuster and the author to continue publishing exceptional books for years to come. We thank you for supporting the author's copyright by purchasing an authorized edition of this book.
No amount of this book may be reproduced or stored in any format, nor may it be uploaded to any website, database, language-learning model, or other repository, retrieval, or artificial intelligence system without express permission. All rights reserved. Inquiries may be directed to Simon & Schuster, 1230 Avenue of the Americas, New York, NY 10020
or permissions@simonandschuster.com.
First Aladdin hardcover edition June 2025
Text © 2025 by Simon & Schuster, LLC
Jacket illustration © 2025 by Laura Catrinella
Also available in an Aladdin paperback edition.
All rights reserved, including the right of reproduction in whole or in part in any form.
ALADDIN and related logo are registered trademarks of Simon & Schuster, LLC.
For information about special discounts for bulk purchases, please contact Simon & Schuster Special Sales at 1-866-506-1949 or business@simonandschuster.com.
Simon & Schuster strongly believes in freedom of expression and stands against censorship in all its forms. For more information, visit BooksBelong.com.
The Simon & Schuster Speakers Bureau can bring authors to your live event.
For more information or to book an event, contact the Simon & Schuster Speakers Bureau at 1-866-248-3049 or visit our website at www.simonspeakers.com.
Jacket design by Karin Paprocki
Interior design by Mike Rosamilia
The text of this book was set in Horley Old Style MT Std.
Manufactured in the United States of America 0525 BVG
2 4 6 8 10 9 7 5 3 1
Library of Congress Cataloging-in-Publication Data
Names: McCullough, Joy, author. | Bybee, Veeda, author.
Title: Leah vs. Art / by Joy McCullough and Veeda Bybee.
Other titles: Leah versus Art
Description: First Aladdin paperback edition. | New York : Aladdin, 2025. | Series: Team awkward ; 2 | Audience term: Preteens | Summary: Sixth-grader Leah's Quiz Bowl competitive spirit jeopardizes both her friendships and her parent-defying scheme to ditch Art Club.
Identifiers: LCCN 2024040888 (print) | LCCN 2024040889 (ebook) |
ISBN 9781665950756 (pbk) | ISBN 9781665950763 (hc) | ISBN 9781665950770 (ebook)
Subjects: CYAC: Middle schools—Fiction. | Schools—Fiction. | Clubs—Fiction. | Friendship—Fiction. | Family life—Fiction. | LCGFT: Novels.
Classification: LCC PZ7.1.M43412 Le 2025 (print) | LCC PZ7.1.M43412 (ebook) | DDC [Fic]—dc23
LC record available at https://lccn.loc.gov/2024040888
LC ebook record available at https://lccn.loc.gov/2024040889

FOR SELAH,
MY FAVORITE CARDINAL
—V. B.

1.

In one quick motion, I unpeel the last strip of packing tape from the moving box labeled LEAH MILLER'S ROOM. It comes off fast, with a loud *riiip!*

I pause for a moment, taking it all in. Everything else has been put away. Maybe this is the last box I'll ever unpack!

Finally I open the cardboard flaps. A whiff of grape-scented markers and the familiar aroma of books—along with a hint of something floral that I can't quite identify—almost brings me back to our old home on Camp Humphreys, the United States Army base in South Korea.

Growing up with my dad in the military, I've moved around a lot. He's an army dentist and has been assigned to a new place every two years since I can remember. But he's a few years away from retiring, and there's a chance this will be our last PCS—that's "permanent change of station," in military terms.

This could be the last time I have to pack up my life and start all over again.

It's taken a couple of months to get the remainder of our things from the move. The last time I saw my stuff, it was summer. I was wearing sandals and shorts. Now the trees have lost their leaves, and we are days into October. I've been in school for over a month now, with my wardrobe of jeans, thick socks, and sweaters.

It's almost nine thirty p.m. and I'm ready for bed, dressed in hot-pink pajamas covered with elves dancing and singing. (It was my mom's very unfortunate choice of pattern for the family Christmas pajamas.) I hate them, but I'm almost out of laundry. This is my bottom-of-the-drawer choice that no one will ever see. But, whatever. I'll just wear them to bed.

"Look, Avery," I say to the calico cat sitting on the neatly made twin bed. "I finally have everything. Maybe those cute sushi sticky notes are in here somewhere."

Yes! My intuition is right. Nestled near the top are sushi-shaped Post-its. A smiling California roll and blushing nigiri piece seem happy to see me again. Not as happy as I am to see them!

I love stationery. It's almost an obsession. Example: I got to choose the name of our family cat, and what did I named her? Avery, after an office-supply store that sells labels, binders, and all things to organize your life. Steven, my sixteen-year-old brother, thought the choice was completely nerdy. But the name Avery stuck, beating out Steven's generic choice: Furball.

I place the sticky notes on my desk next to cups full of color-coded gel pens, then continue to reach into the box and pull out remnants of a past life. A trophy from the elementary school spelling bee, where last year, in fifth grade, I took home first place with the word "instantaneous." Tucked away in a folder labeled ACCOMPLISHMENTS is a certificate of straight As and perfect attendance.

I take a stack of stickers to pass out tomorrow to my new friends in Team Awkward. I think Jojo would like the dog holding a baseball glove. There's a pair of pink ballet slippers for Izzy, and a colorful collection of hearts for Ryan, who loves all things cute.

When I see the hardcover copy of *Baking: From My Home to Yours,* by my favorite chef, Dorie Greenspan, I nearly fall off my bed. "The recipe for World Peace Cookies!" My voice squeaks. "Almost in time for Christmas!"

I'm already I'm feeling the creep of holiday baking. Who says I can't make gingerbread before Halloween?

I glance at the clock on my desk. It's really getting late. I might not have time to cross off everything on today's to-do list.

Mentally organizing my schedule, I tap the box with my fingers. Avery doesn't like the nervous drumming. She walks toward the door, signaling for me to let her out.

I ignore the cat. I still want to add a couple

of paragraphs to my history project. Unpacking really took up more time than I thought.

Avery scratches at the door. She looks at me expectantly.

"Fine." I scoot off the bed. "You win." As I open the door, the sounds of laughter and loud rock music remind me of the party going on downstairs.

My parents are listening to the vinyl records that came with the last of our family boxes. Dad was so excited to have his music collection again that he invited our next-door neighbors, the Walkers, over for a listening party. Thankfully, Ben, their cute son—who is twelve years old, my age—didn't come with his parents. Ben is mixed race like me. He's Black and Lao American, and I'm Thai American and white. Mrs. Walker loves that another Southeast Asian mom moved into the neighborhood. Mom and Mrs. Walker have become fast friends and take trips into DC together to stock up at the Asian grocery stores.

Part of me wanted Ben to hang out tonight, but I'm kind of awkward around him. We're in the same advanced classes, and yet we've barely mumbled hello to each other at school. I'm still hoping there's a chance we'll become friends, though.

Having moved around so much, I've learned how to talk about anything with people I don't know very well. *Except* if your name is Ben Walker. Then I forget everything I know about polite conversation. If you *aren't* the boy next door who metaphorically ties my tongue in knots, I'll try to talk about something that's interesting about you. For example:

"I like the stickers on your water bottle."

"Have you hiked Yosemite?"

"That's a really cool pen! Where did you get it?"

"What do you think of Radiohead? A little spooky, or a lot brilliant?"

Making friends has been easy, but keeping friendships is tricky. Before this move, I didn't have the experience of having a close group of friends, or even a best friend.

Forrest Ridge, Virginia, is different. For starters, we don't live on a military base. I'm going to a regular public middle school. I get to meet kids who stick around longer than one assignment.

I really like this new home and new school.

Meeting Jojo, Izzy, and Ryan in the secret locker room is the best thing that's happened to me in a really long time. Even better than making the QuizBowl team at school this year. Tryouts were the first week of school and I was so nervous. Ryan made me a pin that said YOU GOT THIS in bright, bold letters, and I think the positive reinforcement really did help. I felt confident and knew I had something to offer the QuizBowl team. When qualifying notifications were sent out the following week, I wasn't shocked to make it in but was happy all the same. To make things even better, Izzy also made the team. Practice will be starting soon, and I can't wait.

While the first day at Kagan Middle School started off terrible, meeting Team Awkward made every embarrassing moment worth it. Even if the group name came from cringeworthy experiences, awkwardness was something we all shared. Together, we can own it, share it, and laugh about it.

The music continues to float up from the family room, but Mom will be up soon to tell me to get to bed. I place the cookbook down and pull the last of the things out of my box.

My hands wrap around a book with crinkled pages. The cover feels slick, like it is somehow . . . wet?

I peek into the box and gasp. *No.*

A bottle of essential oil rolls around the now-vacant box. The lid is off, and the bottle is also empty. The oil has leaked out, soaking through one of my cookbooks. Left for months in storage, the pages are now stuck together.

This is where the flower smell is coming from. The essential oil.

Taking deep breaths, I try to separate the paper. There's no use. The ink has already smudged, and no amount of careful prying will help the pages become readable. The book is *ruined*.

Shaking, I place the book on my desk. I don't use essential oils. But I know who does.

I yank my bedroom door open and march halfway down the stairs, just in time to see Mom open the front door and reveal that Ben is standing on our porch. In a normal navy-blue sweatshirt and gray sweatpants. Not hot-pink pajamas with dancing elves.

I groan. *Why me?*

Mistake. Ben looks up.

I want to run back to my room, but my legs feel locked into place. In front of Ben, once again, I'm speechless.

Mrs. Walker comes to the door. "Oh Ben, honey! Everything all right?"

Ben takes his eyes off me and looks at his mom. "I was just wondering when you'd be coming home. The boys are fighting over the top bunk," he says. "They aren't listening to me."

Mrs. Walker picks up her purse. "We better get going," she says to Mom. "It was so fun tonight!"

The adults say their goodbyes, and the entire time, I'm still standing on the stairs. I'm not sure if it took two minutes or twenty for the Walkers to finally leave. Before his mom shuts the door behind her, Ben looks up at me again and gives a small wave.

This releases the powers restricting me in place. I follow my mom into the kitchen and slam the empty bottle of essential oil on the counter.

"How did this get into my box?" My hands

are on my hips. "It destroyed my *Cookies for All Occasions* book. It had the perfect recipe for snickerdoodles. The edges are crispy, but the center is soft and chewy. Now I'll never make those cookies ever again!"

Mom looks over the empty bottle. "Lavender! I loved this one. I wondered where some of my essential oils went."

She thinks for a moment, then lets out an absent-minded laugh. "At the end of the move, we were so tight on time. The last day, I was shoving things into any box I could find. Today I also found a tube of toothpaste packed with the bed linens!"

I throw my hands up. During the move, I made sure to label each box in my room. I also helped color-code the family boxes to show which ones would be for the new primary bedroom, Steven's stink hole of a room, and the various places around the house. My parents completely disregarded my system and order. And Mom doesn't even care.

She puts down a kitchen towel and walks over to me. "You look really stressed." Mom pats my arm, drawing my attention back to the elves on the sleeve. The ones that Ben saw and will probably tell everyone at school about. "Too bad this bottle is gone," Mom says. "Lavender oil is really good for relaxation."

"Mom!" I explode. "You can't just throw things into boxes. Especially *my* box. This stupid oil is all over my books. Now I have to clean up this mess instead of finishing my project tonight."

Mom's face goes from sympathetic to stern in a snap. "Are you up working on homework? At ten o'clock on a school night?"

I motion toward the record player. "No one was going to sleep with all the noise."

Dad comes over with a roll of paper towels. "I can help clean up the mess. You know, I'm sure your project doesn't need any more tinkering. It's probably great as it is."

Mom nods in agreement. Her face is softer now. "Leah, forget about your schoolwork. Come sit down and have some ice cream." She pats a kitchen barstool and goes over to the fridge. "We made brownies with the Walkers, but we forgot to serve the ice cream with them. Oh! We can have chocolate-cherry Coke floats. I'll get the soda and syrup."

"Are you kidding?" I say. "There's no way I am going to eat an ice cream sundae right before bed." *Especially* a float. All that caffeine in the soda will keep me up!

Mom isn't listening. She's already scooping chocolate ice cream into two tall glasses. "Do you want two scoops or one?"

Dad holds out a glass. "I'll take a float."

Just then, Steven comes down the stairs. His floppy black hair falls over his face. "We're having ice cream? Why didn't anyone tell me?"

I feel like screaming. "It isn't good to eat like this before bedtime," I say, trying to keep my voice calm. "Especially all that dairy. Mom, aren't you lactose intolerant?"

Mom is layering hot fudge into the glasses. She adds more ice cream, followed by the soda. She stirs in cherry syrup and passes the floats around. Mom places a spoonful of ice cream in her mouth. "Sometimes it doesn't affect me. Guess I'll find out later tonight."

I cover my face with my hands. "Oh my gosh."

Dad is laughing. He reaches over, prying my fingers away from my eyes. "Come on, Leah," he says. "You're in sixth grade. Rebel a little. You can have some ice cream this late at night. It's what kids your age do."

I shake my hands out of Dad's grip. "Kids my age who want to do well in school are most likely in bed right now. If they are rebelling, it's to stay up late to finish projects like *I* should be. Not having ice cream, and definitely not caffeinated floats."

Steven is holding out a spoon. "I'll take a sundae." He looks at me and shrugs. "I live on the edge."

I shake my head. "My idea of living on the edge is making it to the state finals in QuizBowl."

Mom places her spoon down. "Is this another academic activity?" Her voice has lost some of the playfulness. "Aren't you already in chess club, National Junior Honor Society, and Student Council?"

"Yes," I say. "But no worries. QuizBowl works with my schedule."

Mom taps on the counter with her fingers.

"I think you're involved in too much. And they are all really similar, too. At least have a variety. Maybe play a sport? Let some energy out!"

I take a step back. Sports have *never* been my thing. It's like my parents don't know me. "Mom," I say. "QuizBowl is important. If you start in middle school, you'll have a better shot of making the high school team. At that level, there are scholarships available. It looks really good for college."

Mom frowns. "When did sixth graders start worrying about college?" Then her face brightens, and I get suspicious of the smile across her face. "Oh, *wait*. I almost forgot. We have a surprise for you!" She runs over to what she calls "the everything drawer" (let's be real, it's a junk drawer), pulls out a piece of brightly colored paper, and hands it to me.

I take the paper and read it over. "Art club?"

"Yes!" Mom says, and her smile grows wider. "Mrs. Walker told me about it last week. It's at your school, and they explore painting, ceramics, watercolor. There are two sections, actually." She looks over my shoulder at the flyer. "There's a sculpture section on Monday and general art club on Tuesday. You can choose either one. It doesn't matter."

Mom points to the paper. "It sounds like fun! And guess what? It's all paid for. The Walkers let me know that Ben also signed up." She taps the flyer. "Perfect timing—variety!"

I read over the flyer. The club meets after school in the art room. Mr. Jenner, the art teacher, is the one leading it. Knowing Ben will be in attendance makes it more interesting, but it has one big thing going against it.

"I can't." I put the paper down and push it toward Mom. "The sculpture section is on Mondays when I have chess club. I don't like clay or getting dirty like that anyway. The general art club is on Tuesdays. The same time QuizBowl meets."

Mom slides the flyer back my way. "You don't need to do everything in your first year of middle school. Come on. Try out art club. Maybe this is a sign that QuizBowl can wait."

"No." My voice sounds flat, like how I feel toward Mom's interest in the arts. Mom doesn't get it. I'm not like her. I don't wear funky jewelry or take time in the morning to pick out an outfit that fits my mood. I'm not interested in self-expression through clothing.

I crumple up the flyer to make my point.

Mom uncrumples the paper. Again she slides it over. "Art club will be good for you."

"I just made the QuizBowl team, and I have a shot at being team captain! There's an opening and I want to run."

Mom isn't moved. "You can be team captain next year."

I shake my head. "In the history of QuizBowl at Kagan, there has never been a sixth-grade team captain. This could be historic."

Dad's been quiet this entire time, but now he turns over the crumpled flyer. "This is something you need to do. Not for me, not for Mom. This club will be for you."

"But—" I start to say.

"No buts." Dad holds up his hand. "This conversation is over, Leah. Art club is mandatory. You can keep your other clubs, but you need to do this one."

I close my eyes. I never have a say in anything.

We move every couple of years because of Dad's job. I wear ridiculous pajamas Mom picked out. Now I'm forced to give up QuizBowl because my parents think I need *variety*?

　I turn around in a huff to stomp back up the stairs.

2.

Team Awkward is gathered in our secret locker room for lunch. I'm still amazed no one else in the school knows about this hidden space off the gym. Even though it's a locker room, it's huge.

At school we have something called "Kagan Time" where we can choose different activities during lunch. Instead of everyone eating in the cafeteria, we can go to teachers' classrooms for clubs or homework help. Not having a supervised lunch hour gives us the perfect opportunity to slip away to the secret locker room.

LEAH VS. ART

We've been coming here since the start of school, when we stumbled upon it. Today the locker room looks a little different. A swirl of orange, red, and yellow leaves decorates the walls. "Who put this all up?" I ask as I enter the room. The door is propped open with a book. We've found that we can hear the bell with the door slightly open.

Ryan raises her hand shyly. "Me," she said. "I thought we could use some fall vibes."

I look around the room and admire how she has a talent for making spaces more inviting. Last week, Ryan strung twinkly lights from the ceiling. "You're so creative," I say, sitting down on the bench. I snap the plastic lid off my bento box. "I hate all things art." I already filled them in on my new extracurricular activity when I saw them this morning.

Ryan walks over and steals one of my blueberries. "What's so bad about art?" she says. "That sounds like it could be really fun. If I didn't have to babysit on Tuesdays, I'd sign up too." She goes back to her seat.

"It's the same time as QuizBowl!" I say.

Jojo holds out her hand. "Give me your planner."

I narrow my eyes, looking at the peanut butter on her fingers. "Why?"

"I know you schedule everything," Jojo says. "I want to take a look."

I hand her a napkin and watch carefully as she wipes her hands. After she's peanut-butter-free, I reach into my bag and give her my bullet journal. In this green notebook, I write down my monthly and weekly calendar. Bullet journaling is something Mom and I do together. On Sundays we watch rom-coms and plan out our week. It's probably the one thing we have in common.

Jojo flips through the journal. "Here," she says, pointing to a page. "Art club is tomorrow, but QuizBowl doesn't start till next week Tuesday. Could you alternate between the two?"

Ryan shakes her head. "Leah's parents are paying for art club. It doesn't seem right to have her miss so many days."

Izzy bites into an apple. "It's not right that she is being forced to go."

I look at my friends. An idea is forming. "Jojo is onto something. What if I *pretend* to go to art club? How much am I really missing anyway? Making a collage from magazines? I can do that at home anytime."

"Yes!" Izzy says. "We need your brains to help us in QuizBowl. You can't drop out."

"I think you can pull it off," Jojo replies.

Ryan is quiet. We all look at her. "I don't know, Leah," she says. "It feels a little like lying."

There's a moment of silence. Then I start to laugh, waving my hand in front of me as if I am brushing away the guilt in the air. "I can go to art club every once in a while," I say, my voice reassuring. "For sure the very first one. So technically I will have joined the club. And it's art. How much is there to learn about coloring?"

Ryan looks worried. "You don't just learn how to 'do art.' It's taking the time to develop your own style and find what moves you."

I open my mouth to respond, but from down the hall the lunch bell rings. We have to start packing up. The downside of Team Awkward meeting in the secret locker room is that it's far from the cafeteria and our classrooms. We need to hurry to the next class.

"How about you all come over after school?" I ask. "We can talk this over more at my place. I just got some of my cookbooks. I'll make something."

Everyone quickly texts their parents to check, and they can all come. Ryan, who doesn't have a phone, uses mine. Her mom also agrees.

As we leave the secret locker room, I'm feeling hopeful. I don't have to give up QuizBowl. I just have to fake attending art club. How hard can this be?

3.

The warm scent of sugar and spices greets me and the rest of Team Awkward when we open the front door of my house. "What's baking?" Jojo says.

I hang up my bookbag in the mudroom and shrug. "I have no idea," I answer.

We all take off our shoes. Mom isn't a stickler for most things, but she draws the line at shoes in the house. It's an Asian tradition she enforces, with a sign: LEAVE YOUR WORRIES AND SHOES AT THE FRONT DOOR!

Team Awkward follows me down the hall.

Mom is in the kitchen, sliding cookies onto a wire cooling rack.

Jojo is the first one to pull out a barstool. "Hey, Mrs. Miller," she says. "What's cooking?"

There are two plates of cookies on the counter. All are golden in color, covered with a light dusting of cinnamon and sugar. The sugar crystals sparkle in the afternoon light.

I look up at Mom. "Wait, are these—"

"Snickerdoodles!" Mom says. She looks around the kitchen. "Hi, girls! So glad you all came over. You can test this batch right out of the oven. Izzy, I also made gluten-free ones. They are on the pink plate."

Everyone eagerly takes a cookie. I grab a snickerdoodle and bend it in half. It's soft, yet crisp and crunchy on the edges. Just like snickerdoodles are supposed to be. I take a bite. It's perfect.

"Mom! These are so good," I say with my mouth full of cookie. "How many times did you practice the recipe?"

Mom gives me a funny look. "Practice? This is my first time making them. Even the gluten-free ones."

I swallow. Mom isn't known for following directions. She sometimes likes to wing things. Like making spur-of-the-moment Coke floats and adding a loose bottle of essential oil to a not-quite-full box of someone else's belongings. This impulsiveness could be a disaster for baking.

"Wow," I say with surprise. "They turned out great for a first-time recipe."

Mom laughs. "You act like I don't know how to bake. I've been cooking for a while. Once you understand how it's done, other recipes will be familiar. It's all about feel."

"Feel?" I question. "What do you mean?"

Mom sits down next to me. "Like, you know when it's done because the house starts to smell like cookies. Or the tops are turning light brown, and you know it's time to take them out of the oven. It's an instinct, I suppose." She winks. "This intuition is something art club will help with. Trusting your gut."

Everyone in the room is quiet. Ryan looks down at the counter. To swallow my guilt, I take another bite.

Mom grabs a bag off the counter and hands it

to me. "Here," she says. "I got you something."

I reach into the bag and pull out a brand-new copy of *Cookies for All Occasions*.

"I dropped by the bookstore this morning and picked it up," Mom explains.

I slowly open the book. There are no hints of lavender in the pages. Instead it gives off a new-book smell of paper and ink. The book has the glorious feeling of crisp, fresh pages that need to be touched and studied. I cradle the cookbook in my arms.

"Thank you, Mom." I regret my huffiness last night. "I'm sorry."

Mom smiles. "I'm sorry for ruining your book."

Maybe Mom knows a little bit about me after all.

I always thought baking was a lot like schoolwork. It takes more than the first try to master a subject. But maybe there's something else to understand with these snickerdoodles, and Mom's gesture.

I brush this idea off. A few cookies aren't going to make up for mandatory art club. Mom may know some of my heart, but if she took time to truly understand all of me, she'd see why QuizBowl is important. Why I'm going to make it happen.

Mom looks around the quiet room. "I better go. You all seem like you have a lot to talk about without me here."

Jojo smiles up at Mom, while Ryan can't look her in the eye.

"Thanks, Mrs. Miller, for the cookies," Izzy says. "I see where Leah gets her baking."

I want to correct Izzy and tell her I get it from Dorie Greenspan and not my absent-minded mother. "These cookies are really great," I say instead. "Thanks, Mom."

Mom hands me the now-familiar crumpled-up flyer. "Take some cookies with you to art club tomorrow."

I smile, a little too wide. "Definitely."

4.

After school the next day, I'm the first one to walk through the art club doors. Team Awkward helped me work out a plan. I've committed. I will go to the first art club meeting to get a feel for it, and so I'll have believable details to share with my parents if they ask how it's going. Next week I'll go to QuizBowl.

There are chairs pushed against those large rectangular tables made for shared spaces. Out of habit, I sit right up front. I open up my backpack and pull out my pencil bag. Most of the supplies are already provided, but I wanted to bring a few things of my own just in case. I place the bag, a handwoven pouch made in Thailand, right on the table. My grandmother got it for me when she went back last year, and I love the intricate patterns that line this zippered bag.

After unzipping my pouch, I lay out a ruler, erasers, and a collection of freshly sharpened graphite and charcoal pencils. I didn't know charcoal was used for anything besides fuel for a grill, but here I am ready to draw with it. Supposedly, these materials are good for "blending," some kind of artsy-fartsy terminology.

I turn the pencils over so they all face up. One rolls off the table and falls to the floor. This slight clatter draws the attention of Mr. Jenner, the art club teacher, who was stapling motivational posters to a bulletin board across the room.

He starts to walk over. "Hi!" he says with enthusiasm. "Welcome to art club."

I give a small wave. "Hi."

I study his T-shirt. It's olive green, with a single red star across the front. Something about the design looks familiar. I make a mental note to do an internet search on the image.

It doesn't surprise me that Mr. Jenner is wearing some kind of vintage-looking T-shirt. His glasses also look a little retro. He's white, with a slightly scruffy brown beard. This is my first time meeting him, but Mr. Jenner has a reputation for being a favorite teacher and a cool dad. His son is an eighth grader at our school. If he's as chill as everyone claims he is, I'm banking on the fact that he doesn't take attendance in this club too seriously.

Automatically, I do not like Mr. Jenner. I've had enough of hip parents who listen to indie rock. They are the reason why I'm in this situation. Give me the awkward, uptight adult any day. I know how to vibe with that crowd.

Mr. Jenner shifts back and forth in his high-top Converse sneakers. I think my studying of his outfit is making him uncomfortable. He clears his throat and looks at a clipboard in his hands. "So, what's your name?"

"Leah Miller," I answer. Someone slides into the seat next to me.

I glance over, and it's Ben. The stuffy feeling of the art room evaporates, and the mood feels lighter.

"Hey," he says. He pulls out a sketchbook and a pen.

"Hey," I reply, trying my best to match his tone. I push a pencil back and forth on the table. It slips out of my grip and tumbles to the ground. As I reach over to get it, Ben does the same. Our fingers brush when he hands me my pencil. Instantly, my face feels hot. I quickly put the pencil back on the table.

I sit up straight and focus on Mr. Jenner.

"Yes, I'm Leah." Thankfully, my voice sounds normal. "This is my first time."

Mr. Jenner checks my name off the list. "First time in art club here at Kagan?"

I shake my head. "No, first time doing art."

Mr. Jenner pauses and pushes up the glasses on his nose. He looks amused. "You don't think you've ever created art before?"

I meet his eyes, something I know most kids my age wouldn't do to a teacher or authority figure. Here's his first chance to see that I am not most kids. "If you mean the stick figures we do in elementary, or macaroni necklaces strung together in preschool, sure," I say. "I've *crafted*. But anything art, I've been exempt."

Mr. Jenner looks taken aback. Either at my boldness in speech, or the fact that I haven't broken eye contact the entire time. He holds the clipboard close to his chest. "I don't think I've ever heard anyone say they've been exempt from *art*."

"It's factual," I reply. "During art in fourth and fifth grade, I got permission to study in the science room at my old school. I also helped sort library books."

Mr. Jenner studies me closely. "Where did you go to school?"

"Overseas in South Korea," I say. "My family is in the military."

Talking about my life at Camp Humphreys makes my heart miss it all over again. Even though I'm used to moving a lot, it doesn't get any easier. I didn't think it was possible for happy and sad to coexist at the same time, but it is.

I'm hoping to stay in Forrest Ridge for a long time, but I do miss the friends and life I left behind. Plus, starting over is hard. I have to speak up each time I go somewhere new, or else I fade into the background. As much as I like Virginia and going to school at Kagan, I still feel a little untethered.

Like I'm not quite grounded and still trying to find my footing.

Mr. Jenner taps the clipboard on my desk. "Glad to have you with us, Ms. Miller. I hope you will find your creative self this semester."

He leaves and continues to check attendance around the room.

Once he is out of earshot, I turn to Ben. "Is your mom forcing you to do art club too?"

"No." Ben looks surprised. "Is this some kind of punishment for you?"

I take in the boy that is Ben Walker. Black hair cut short. His outfit is jeans and a T-shirt. I blink. It's not just any T-shirt. I recognize the graphic on the front. Ben's black shirt has a white outline of a triangle on the front, and a rainbow going through it. This is from a Pink Floyd album cover. A hip music T-shirt. A realization dawns on me. I didn't notice this before, but Ben is cool. It seems like I judged him too quickly before.

"Oh," I say. I can't keep the disappointment out of my voice. "You're one of those."

Ben looks at me strangely. "One of those . . . who like art?"

All my nervousness around him evaporates. Now that I know what kind of guy he is, we probably won't be friends. Or anything more than that. Ben will like music that I've never heard of, watch films that are obscure, and read books written by old white men that are considered classics. Everything pretentious and snobby. Basically, he's twenty years away from becoming my parents.

"Everyone has their thing," I say with a shrug. "Art isn't one of mine."

I can almost hear the next question on the tip of his tongue, but Mr. Jenner is standing at the front of the room.

"Unless you think you're in the wrong place, welcome to art club!" He says this without looking my way, but I feel like that was directed at me.

Mr. Jenner passes out a syllabus, which is impressive. This shows signs of organization, which doesn't always exist for creative people. I can't remember the last time Mom brought a shopping list to the grocery store. Once she tried meal planning for a week, but the commitment to

Meatless Monday and Taco Tuesday paralyzed her. Instead we had grilled cheese and cold cereal for dinner every night that week.

"This first section, we're focused on drawing," Mr. Jenner says. "Throughout our time in art club, we will explore different mediums of art and learn how creation is a form of expression. If you ever want to join the sculpture section, this happens on Monday. Go anytime. For art club, there will be daily prompts, which I'll post in our shared online classroom."

I glance over the schedule, figuring out if there are any days that won't be totally miserable so I can try to line up my brief appearances. I'm definitely skipping the watercolor days. I also cross out the weeks we work on collage and modern art.

Mr. Jenner passes out sheets of paper. "For today's assignment, we will use pens to sketch."

I look at my pencils, all neat in a row. The thought of not being able to erase sends me into a panic. "Can I use a pencil? No one does anything perfect the first time."

"Exactly!" Mr. Jenner bangs his hand on the

table in excitement. "Today we want to create without holding ourselves back. Don't worry about erasing. Just draw and see."

I lean forward. "Are you going to give us a basic lesson on sketching? Or just a pep talk about how anyone can draw and it's all just a series of shapes and lines?"

Mr. Jenner hands me a pen. "Sounds like you just motivated us all."

I frown at the writing utensil in my hand. "I haven't studied for this."

Ben turns toward me. In fact, *everyone* is looking at me. "This is art *club*. There aren't any grades or anything to study," he says.

Mr. Jenner claps his hands together, drawing the focus back to him. "I do have some help," he says. "Let's start with a prompt. Anyone have a suggestion?"

A girl in the back raises her hand. It's Moira Harper. "Yes." She looks right at me. "Loud."

Moira told the whole middle school on the first day of school that she saw Jojo's underwear. Jojo is right. Moira is the worst.

I choose to ignore her crusty glare and my hand

shoots up. "That's too vague," I say, before Mr. Jenner can even call on me. "Can't you be more specific? Like, people, place, or animal?"

Mr. Jenner is getting ready to set a timer. "This isn't Pictionary, but sure. Use one of those. This is a speed drawing. I'll give you all ten minutes. Starting now!" He starts a timer on his phone.

Ten minutes! I find myself taking short, quick breaths. Am I really hyperventilating over drawing? Mom said this exercise was supposed to be relaxing and freeing.

I turn to complain to Ben, but he's already bent over his paper.

I pop off my pen cap and press the sharp point into the paper. A blob of black ink puddles out, spreading like a stain.

"No!" I gasp.

Students around me groan. I don't blame them.

Ugh. I will forever be known as Loud Girl. *Thanks a lot, Moira.* I try to slow down my breathing and remember that art club isn't my main goal. QuizBowl is.

Once again, Mr. Jenner is by my side. "Are you okay?"

"My pen leaked," I say sheepishly. "Can I get another paper?"

Mr. Jenner studies the dark spot on my white paper. "That is a cool shape. What do you think it looks like?"

"It doesn't look like anything," I say with exasperation. "I have a broken pen. I made a mistake."

Mr. Jenner stares at my splatter like it's a Rorschach inkblot test. (That's an evaluation that claims to determine who you are by what images you see in a smudge of ink. *And* it's been seriously criticized, by the way.) He pushes the paper toward me. "Okay, then. What can you make out of this mistake?"

I look closer and see nothing but ink. It really spread across the paper, like limbs branching out. "I don't know. Maybe a big tree."

"I like it." Mr. Jenner looks pleased. "Go from there."

I study this so-called tree. With my pen, I draw lines off the treelike inkblot. They are knobby and wonky. My tree looks like something a second grader made. I glance over at Ben.

Using small lines and shading, he's sketched out a dragon with a long body like a serpent and a fiery mane around its head. "Is that a naga?" I whisper, trying my best not to be loud.

Ben looks over in bewilderment. "Yes," he says. "How do you know?"

I push my pencil pouch over to him. "You see these spiral coils woven in? They are nagas. My grandma from Thailand told me how statues of nagas line the staircases to Buddhist temples. They are protectors or something."

Ben nods. "Yes, my mom says they protect the cities in Laos. They live in the water. I've been really into drawing them lately."

"Laos and Thailand are neighboring countries," I say. "So it makes sense that they share the same mythical creatures."

The buzzer on the phone rings. I haven't drawn very much. I panic and start to scribble any shape that pops into my head, only laying my pen down when Mr. Jenner is in front of my table, collecting our work.

With magnets, he hangs our drawings on the chalkboard so everyone can see them. There are illustrations of storms. Yelling people. I'm the only one with a tree. I feel so exposed. My piece is the worst.

"All right," Mr. Jenner says. "Come to the front of the room and let's take a closer look at everyone's piece. In minute we will discuss. Look for the positives and tell us what you think."

Normally, I feel just fine having my work on display. I wrote an essay for Earth Day last year on the noise pollution of military aircraft around Okinawa. Right now I feel a little shaky. Art is a completely different subject. I walk to the front of the room and study the drawings by my fellow students. Their pictures look so much better than mine. Moira has drawn a galloping horse, with hooves blurring into clouds of dust. I know it's her work because of the big, swoopy "Moira" signature at the bottom of the page. It looks as if the horse will run right off the page and into the classroom. It's irritating that such a beautiful sketch can come from someone who is so terrible. I'm suddenly in front of my piece.

A blond girl stands next to me. "I like how you made that blob a cluster of leaves. I never thought of a tree being loud, but it really is."

A boy next to her nods in agreement. "Yeah. Like, they don't say anything at all, but their large presence looms around us. That kind of grandeur can't be ignored."

"Yup. That's what I was going for. Loud, silent trees," I say, but inside I'm cringing. I was so focused on salvaging my paper, I completely forgot about the "loud" prompt. I drew whatever shape I could get out of my ink blob.

These art kids are something else. They see something in nothing.

Or maybe they're just making it all up because they feel sorry for me. I've never had pity like this before. Being an art club charity case might feel worse than being labeled Loud Girl.

Mr. Jenner hands us back our drawings. I slide it into my sketchbook. When we're dismissed, I am the first one out the door, just like I was the first one through it. Hopefully, my first day of art club will also be my last.

5.

A week goes by, and it's time for the Great Plan to commence. Today is Tuesday official day one of QuizBowl, and pretend day two of art club.

Despite my loathing of art, I am ever the dutiful student, so of course I still did our "homework" for art club this week. I had to draw in my sketchbook every day for ten minutes. The daily prompts were posted on our club online classroom, and I followed these daily reminders.

Unsure of what to draw, I continued my theme of the blobby tree. The tree dancing, the tree napping . . . and for the "wave" prompt, the tree boogie-boarding. Part of me feels a tiny thrill of excitement at thinking so freely. A larger section of my brain, the more practical side, knows that I'm just making stuff up. It's an easy but somehow challenging assignment, and I'm just happy to have it done.

At lunch I meet Team Awkward in the secret locker room. JoJo and Izzy are sharing a package of cheese crackers. Ryan is sitting on the bench, sewing a patch on a jean jacket.

I hand her the spiral-bound book. "I know you aren't in art club, but you have class with Mr. Jenner, right? Can you show this to him? I want to get credit."

"You know art club is a fun after-school activity, right?" Ryan says, opening the sketchbook. "You aren't graded."

Izzy gets up and comes over to Ryan. "I want to see!" she says, and attempts to get my book.

I let out a yelp and snatch the book away. "You can't look at it!"

Izzy takes her hand back in surprise. "Why not? You're showing it to everyone in art club. You won't even be there."

I sit down on the bench and pull out my bento box from my backpack. I start to unpack my lunch. "Exactly. It can be judged when I'm not around. I don't think I can take anyone looking at these drawings right in front of me. Let them look while I'm seeking the nomination for QuizBowl captain."

Izzy grins. "You know you have my vote. You'll probably win by a landslide. I heard from an eighth grader that most people don't want to be captain. Too much pressure. I don't think you'll have much competition." She makes a grab for my sketchbook again. I hold my artwork out of her reach. "We won't know for sure unless we can see what you drew," Izzy says.

Jojo sighs with impatience. "Come on," she says. "It's just us."

Ryan puts a hand on my arm. "She's right. We are your safe space. Nothing you show us will be embarrassing."

I brush my hair away from my face. "I'm—I'm just not a good artist," I stammer. "In my mind, I have something great. I try to put it on paper, and it's not at all what I pictured."

I sigh and flip open the book to prove my point. I motion to a drawing. "What does this look like to you?"

Ryan looks closely at the paper. "A tree."

A little rush of triumph flows through me. She could tell what it was. Maybe I'm not such a bad artist after all. I give Ryan my sketchbook. "You recognize it? I had a mishap in art, but I was able to make a tree out of this blob of ink."

"Yes." She smiles encouragingly. "Maybe you can add Lovebug underneath the leaves. He would make a great cameo."

Lovebug is the stray cat we found wandering the halls of Kagan Middle School during a school lockdown. He's a Savannah cat, a breed that's larger than most domesticated cats. The school thought we had a wild bobcat roaming the halls. The four of us bonded over being stuck in the secret locker room while everyone else in the school was sheltering from the alleged bobcat. Turned out it was just Lovebug. Who is as sweet as can be.

His owner never claimed him. After a few days, Ryan convinced her parents to adopt him.

Lovebug has been our unofficial Team Awkward mascot ever since.

Jojo takes to the book and flips to another sketch. "Is this another blob tree, and an . . . elephant?"

Any confidence I had about my drawing abilities quickly leaves. "No. It's supposed to be a horse. Don't you see the cowboy hat on the tree?"

Izzy reaches for the book and holds it up to her face. "Oh, I thought that was just more leaves."

I take back my book. "It's for the word 'wild.' That day's drawing prompt."

Izzy continues analyzing the picture. "I still don't get it."

"As in, the Wild West," I say. "The tree is a forest sheriff or something."

JoJo blinks. "A forest sheriff . . . ?" Her shoulders start to shake, as if she's holding something in. Izzy presses her lips together. A snort escapes, and she buries her head in her hands. Even Ryan, the kindest one in our group, covers her mouth with a book. The moment of silence breaks, and they all erupt with laughter.

Their laughing seems to bounce off the wall

of the locker room. It's magnified in this small space. I sit still, dread prickling my body like an itchy sweater. These girls don't really know me, and I don't really know them. I'm new all over again and don't belong anywhere. "I don't have time for this," I say, putting away the bento box. I pick up my backpack. "I'm going to be late for class."

We all know there are still ten minutes left of lunch. I dash out of the room anyway.

The last bell rings and I linger for a few minutes in science. I wanted to see my teacher about a grade change, but there are several students in front of me. The minutes go by, and I glance at my cell phone. There goes my wish to get to QuizBowl early. I had plans to chat up the advisor and make a good first impression. Now, if I am lucky, I might make it into the room before it starts. I ditch the line and walk away, but then I pick up my pace and start to run. I'm going to be out of breath and sweaty—so much for a positive initial appearance. Izzy sees me in the hall. "Hey!" she yells. "We've been texting you.

You haven't answered anything on our Team Awkward thread."

I'm pumping my arms and panting. I hate being late for things. "Hurry!" I yell back to Izzy, not answering her questions. She's steps behind me. "We might make it before it starts."

I reach the classroom door and throw it open just in time to see Ms. Levari already at the front of the room, passing out papers.

I slide into an empty seat. Izzy finds a chair next to me. Ms. Levari doesn't look up from her papers. "You're both late," she says to us. "Consider this your warning. Next time you show up tardy, don't come at all."

Izzy's cheeks flush. I bet my face is red too.

Then I look around the room, and my heart rate starts to go back to normal. This is an environment that I thrive in. Kids sit attentively at desks, unlike the creative chaos that was art club last week. A respectful silence fills the room as we wait for instruction. Here I know the rules. No one will laugh at me in QuizBowl.

Ms. Levari hands me a schedule. Seeing the Times New Roman twelve-point font and bullet-point outline is like being reunited with an old friend. Mr. Jenner's syllabus for art club was fine. It wasn't like he used Comic Sans. But the QuizBowl handout is more detailed, with sidebar info and a study schedule that I can't wait to color-code into my planner.

I look over the timeline. We have five tournaments, with the last leading up to district finals. During regular season, we compete against the top middle schools in our region. Our biggest rival, Finston Prep, a private school in a neighboring town, is up first.

On the handout is a breakdown of how Quiz-Bowl works:

QuizBowl is a question-and-answer game with two competing teams. Each team is made up of five players. The questions cover subjects including math, science, pop culture, language arts, and more. Contestants buzz in and have twelve seconds to answer math questions or anything else that needs computing with paper and pencil. They have seven seconds to answer all other trivia questions. Each competition has a total of two ten-minute rounds, with a ten-minute break in between the rounds.

Ms. Levari is standing at the front of the room. "Today we will pick a team captain," she says with authority. "The only required responsibility of the team captain is to answer the bonus question in case of a tie." She paces the room with hands clasped behind her back. "However, behind the scenes, this leader is the one who holds the group together. The captain will help organize and coordinate practice times."

She looks each one of us square in the face. "They must be dedicated, and a good motivator. A good team does not criticize or tear each other down. This captain will be the one leading the support. A lot of responsibility will fall to the captain. Choose someone who is dedicated."

Out of the corner of my eye, I try to get a feel for the other students in the room. We need six to make a team. Five to play, and one alternate. We have just the right number of students here. I notice a boy who looks familiar. Even though I didn't think I was ready to speak to Izzy just yet, I can't help but turn in her direction. "Is that Luke?" I say quietly.

Izzy looks toward him, and her eyes widen.

"Yes," she whispers. Luke is the boy she got stuck to on the first day of school. She fell into him and managed to snag her braces on his shirt. I'm not sure if they've talked since the time they went to the nurse's office to get unstuck.

Remembering one of the incidents that brought Team Awkward together makes me soften toward Izzy and the other girls. "Forest sheriff" *is* kind of funny. I guess.

"We have QuizBowl scheduled after school on Tuesdays," Ms. Levari continues. "If you really want to succeed, I suggest meeting up at least one other time during the week. Most competitive teams practice for four to six hours a week. The first QuizBowl match will be held in November here at Kagan. To ease the pressure, the PTO has volunteered to host. Your team needs to do nothing but try your best."

Her smile feels less friendly and more polite. "Let's go over QuizBowl expectations. One tip for mastering the information is to study current topics. Do not focus on last year's study packets, although we will spend time on those as well. I will also throw in questions from high school and college QuizBowl packets to make sure you have a well-rounded understanding."

She starts to write categories on the chalkboard. "At minimum, you will want to know the recent Nobel Prize winners, leaders of major countries, relevant Supreme Court rulings, and important senators and governors."

I look around the room. Some students seem to be nervous at the thought of learning college-level material. Ms. Levari hands out slips of paper. "Now, please write your nominations for team captain and pass the names up."

I have no hesitancy about nominating myself. I know Izzy will also write my name down. Maybe this will be a complete shutout.

We give Ms. Levari our votes and she unfolds them into two piles on her desk. "We have just two nominations for team captain," she says. "Derek Knolls and Leah Miller."

She looks at a boy with red hair wearing a buttoned-up polo. "Derek, come take your place in the front and let the team know why you should be captain."

Derek scoots his chair back. He runs a hand through his hair. He's a seventh grader. Tall and a bit awkward, like he's growing into his limbs. He reminds me a little of the blob tree I've been drawing.

"I know I'll be a good captain because I'm, uh, a good leader." Derek shoves his hands in his pockets. "That's it."

Ms. Levari's face is expressionless. "You may have a seat. Ms. Miller?"

I smooth down my skirt. Derek is toast.

Determination washes over me. I want to prove to myself, to Mom and Dad, what I've got. I'm the one who will take our team to the top. I have passion. Enough passion to lie about going to art club and come to QuizBowl instead.

I stand at the front. "We will win the state championship not because of me," I say, "but through teamwork. I believe in each of you. You all are winners. I will be your biggest cheerleader and help us do what it takes to win. If you doubt, I'll be there to help you remember your greatness. We got this!"

I raise my fist in the air. "Also, we can meet at FroGo Café for an extra practice during the week. It's a frozen yogurt shop. It's the one right across the street from the school with the green-and-white striped umbrellas out front. My brother, Steven, works there and will give us a discount."

In the front row, Izzy whoops. "Yeah, Leah!"

The other kids clap. "Frozen yogurt for the win!" someone says.

Ms. Levari passes out our packet study guides. She also gives us strips of paper to write our votes. She collects the papers and clears her throat. "This year's QuizBowl team captain is Leah Miller."

Izzy is giving me a side hug and I feel like confetti is falling from the classroom ceiling in celebration. I walk over to Derek. He looks defeated. I reach out to shake his hand. "First yogurt is on me," I say. "You did well."

"Really?" he says, lighting up a little. "Thanks."

The team spends the next few minutes talking about our practice schedule and study materials. I get everyone's phone number and start a group text. "I'm texting you the address to FroGo Café. I'll see you there on Friday."

Izzy and I leave Ms. Levari's room. We walk down the hallway with arms linked. "You were amazing!" Izzy says.

I can't stop smiling. "I'm the QuizBowl captain!"

Just then, a teacher walks by us. "Leah Miller!"

I look up and come face-to-face with Mr. Jenner. I stop in the hallway.

"Missed you in art club," Mr. Jenner says.

"I had something come up," I mumble. Unlike the first day of art club, I can barely look him in the eye.

He shrugs. Mr. Jenner doesn't look offended that something else took priority over his club. He's a cool teacher. They don't get bothered by things like this. "No problem," he says. "I'll see you next time."

Izzy and I are still linked together. We hurry down the hallway, making our way toward the doors as fast as we can.

"Oh, Leah!" Mr. Jenner shouts from down the hall. "Our prompt for today is 'secrets.' You can draw or work in any medium you like. Today we worked with acrylics."

I look over at my friend in shock. It's like my art teacher knows exactly what I'm doing.

"Can't wait to see what Blob Tree does with this one," Izzy says.

I keep my gaze forward. "Yeah. Me either."

6.

I glance down at my phone. Everyone but Derek is waiting in front of FroGo Café. Izzy and Luke are actually chatting. I feel proud that my friend can talk to him after their first-day fiasco. The rest of the QuizBowl team looks longingly into the windows, peering at the line of frozen yogurt machines.

"When are we going to get some yogurt?" Luke says.

"Yeah," Izzy agrees. "Can't we go inside and wait for him there? With our food?"

Izzy is one of my closest friends, but I can't

show favoritism. Especially when it looks like she's speaking up to be on Luke's side. I shake my head. "We are a team. We enter the store together. Eat together. Win QuizBowl together."

I'm trying to create unity, and Derek is completely ruining my first team-building exercise. If I don't think of something to fill this time of waiting, I may start to lose the excitement of our first QuizBowl outing. Luckily, Derek finally pedals up on a bike.

"Sorry," he says, removing his helmet. "I couldn't find my study packet for the week."

"Don't worry," I say. I reach into my bookbag and pull out a stack of papers. "I have extras."

The rest of the group looks impressed. Good. This show of preparation will win back some trust I lost while we suffered outside waiting. I gesture toward the front door. "After you," I say to Derek. "Yogurt is on me today, remember?"

Derek smiles and wipes the sweat from his forehead. He's the first one through the doors and in line for the yogurt machines.

I spot my brother, Steven, wearing his uniform: purple polo shirt and black visor. He gives me a salute and says, "Welcome to FroGo!" with exaggerated pep.

We each go through the line to get our treat. I grab a paper bowl and make my usual combo: original tart yogurt, sliced fresh strawberries, and strawberry boba balls. Some people like to try new things while eating out. Not me. If I find something I like—for example, plain yogurt and strawberry toppings—I stick to it like glue. Why risk being disappointed when something new falls apart? Cling to the things you know that work.

I hand Steven some money. "Derek's yogurt is on me. Friends and family discount for us all, right?"

Steven winks and shakes a jar on the counter. "Don't forget to tip your favorite frozen yogurt employee."

Once everyone else pays for their (discounted!) yogurt, we snag a table outside. The store is filled with middle and high school kids, and the only seating is on the patio underneath the umbrellas. It's a nice October afternoon, so it's not too chilly to eat frozen dessert outside. I'd much rather be in the store, though. I make a mental note to come earlier next time, or to at least have someone save seats while we order. I want the controlled environment inside. Less distraction from passing cars and pedestrians.

After a few minutes of eating, we pull out our study guides. "Did everyone bring something to write on?" I say, and I plop a bright pink spiral-bound notebook on the table. Everyone has something to write on, except Derek. I don't know why he even bothered to run for team captain. I pull sheets out from the back of my notebook and hand them to him, along with a pencil.

"I read that the best way to study for QuizBowl is to write down the questions," I say. "Let's take ten minutes and see how many questions we can write down. After the time is up, we can go around and ask each other."

Derek raises a hand. "What about the 'Gotta Know' list?"

I'm impressed. I wasn't going to bring up this list of QuizBowl facts until next practice. Maybe I underestimated Derek. "Thank you for mentioning it," I say, and hold out my phone. "I'm sending you all a link to the QuizBowl website.

There is a section on recommended—or 'Gotta Know'—information. If we finish early, maybe we can look over these summaries."

With frozen yogurt in our bellies and a championship on our minds, the Kagan QuizBowl team gets to work. I pull out my different pen colors and start writing. This is the part of studying that I love. Organizing my thoughts. I write the questions in one color, and the answers in another.

We take turns asking each other the questions. In my preparation to be QuizBowl team captain, I read that in addition to writing down the facts, speaking the words out loud helps you retain information.

Izzy reads off the study guide. "Question," she says. "'This baroque artist, famous for his painting *Girl with a Pearl Earring*, is thought to have used a camera obscura, a darkened room with a small lens for projecting an image, to help with his artwork.'"

Luke raises his hand. "Answer: Johannes Vermeer."

Izzy gives him a high five. "Correct!"

I turn toward Derek. "Your turn," I say. "Question: 'A mineral found in kimberlites, it has one of the highest hardness levels on the Mohs' scale and one of the highest thermal conductivities.'"

Derek bites on his nails. "Oh!" he says, lighting up. "I remember. Diamonds."

We go through these rounds for the next hour, and even get a chance to review some of the "Gotta Know" sections. We finish practice just as the parents arrive for pickup.

We go around and give each other fist bumps. "Way to go," I say, as everyone packs up. "If our first practice is a sign of things to come, we are in a good place."

Everyone says goodbye and we promise to ask each other more practice questions on the group text thread. By the time we finish, Steven is off his shift. I meet him out front to catch a ride home. Mom and Dad knew I would be hanging out at the FroGo after school today. They don't know that's because of QuizBowl. As I buckle up in the front seat of his car, he takes off his FroGo black visor and shoves it on my head.

"Gross!" I say, and yank it off. "It's all sticky. What, did you swim in frozen yogurt?"

Steven laughs and pulls out of the parking

lot. "The machine with the Chocolate Cookie Crumble flavor got stuck and spurted all over me."

Steven pretends to wipe a hand on me. I scoot closer to the passenger door. "Stop it!" I laugh. Even though he's big-brother bugging me, I'm feeling good from our practice. "If you don't quit, I'll tell everyone to stop tipping you."

Steven looks my way and grins. "You wouldn't dare lose the discount. Sounds like practice was good."

"It was," I say with a smile. I think of Luke and Izzy talking, and all the questions we answered. "We got a solid team."

Steven slaps the steering wheel with a hand. "I knew it. I'm your good-luck charm."

"So," Steven says. His eyes are straight ahead on the road. "What's going on? Are you skipping art club for QuizBowl?"

I turn to him in shock. "How did you know?"

My brother laughs. "I was there when Mom and Dad were talking with you about art club! You've also been extremely nice to me lately. I knew something was up."

I groan and slump down into the seat. "This is what I get for trying to be kind."

Steven drums his fingers on his chin. "Your secret is safe with me."

"Really?"

"Sure." He shrugs. "Your friends leave good tips."

A song we both know comes on over the car speakers. Steven turns the radio up and we both sing along. We can't have parents who are obsessed with music and not have it rub off on us a little.

At a stoplight, I take Steven's work visor and place it back on his head. "Tell you what," I say. "You keep hooking us up with yogurt, keep quiet on QuizBowl, and I'll keep bringing in the business."

"Deal," Steven says.

We slap hands together in a sibling handshake. I can't wait to see how we do next time.

7.

With FroGo as our extra practice QuizBowl location, our team is meeting twice a week. Each Tuesday, we go after school to Ms. Levari's room. On Fridays, we walk across the street from the school to FroGo. All these practices are helping the QuizBowl team get better. On Halloween, there is a dress-up day at school. Our school mascot is a northern cardinal, the state bird of Virginia. Male cardinals are a brilliant scarlet red, one of our school colors. In honor of our mascot, we all wear matching red shirts and go as the Kagan QuizBowl team.

I've missed every art club since the first one, and I try not to think about that too much. QuizBowl is going really well. The team knows the facts, and our study sessions are paying off. I can almost feel the win in our hands, I know it's so close.

I'm sending daily quiz questions on our text thread and reminding everyone about good study habits. I don't know if there has ever been a more dedicated team captain in all of Kagan Middle School history. Maybe this year we can go undefeated. Last night I dreamed that I was giving a victory speech after crushing district finals. I was dressed in the Kagan colors of scarlet and gold, holding a shiny trophy that was almost bigger than my head. In my dream, I ran up to the stage, past my parents, who were cheering me on. Past my team members and, for some reason, Ben Walker. He was holding out flowers for me and wearing a T-shirt with my face on it. Which is strange because that doesn't seem very cool of him to do.

I can't wait to share this dream with Izzy today. My dream is a little silly, but Izzy would understand. She tells me all about Luke. It's been great to have a friend to share these things with.

It's one p.m. on a Saturday and I have Mom drop me off at FroGo. We just met yesterday after school but I felt like we needed more time to study. With our first match coming up, I called a special weekend practice round.

"Give Steven this," Mom says, and hands me a ten-dollar bill. "He could use a good tip."

"How about 'brush your hair' for a tip?" I say.

Mom laughs. "I'll pick you up after I run my errands," she says. "Have fun!"

I wave goodbye. Mom thinks I'm hanging out friends. She doesn't realize that my idea of fun is secretly practicing with the Kagan Cardinals Quiz-Bowl team.

When I open the door to FroGo, it's packed. I see Izzy, Derek, and other team members already there. I'm still on time, but with Mom's carefree schedule and non-urgency to get out the door, I'm the last of our team to arrive.

I walk up to everyone, put my game face on, and get to work being team captain.

I direct some of the team to the yogurt machines and tell Izzy to find tables. She scowls when I put her on this job. "Why do I have to save seats?" she says.

"We all need to sit together," I say. "It's starting to look a little crowded."

Sure enough, I glance around the room and only a few open tables are left. We grab two small tables by the windows and push them together to make enough space for our group of six.

Glancing around the store, I spot a group of kids wearing matching maroon sweatshirts. Peering closer, I see the words FINSTON PREP QUIZ-BOWL printed in block lettering across the front of each sweatshirt. Izzy looks to see what I'm squinting at.

"No way!" She leans forward. "Is that the first team we're competing against? Do you think they are any good?"

A few of them get up to stand in the frozen yogurt line. I push my chair back. "I'll see what I can find out."

Izzy runs up next to me. "I'm coming with you."

We stand right behind the team. Close enough to hear conversation, but not on top of them to invade their space. A girl with multiple earrings and braided black hair waits in line with an empty cup. When it's her turn at the yogurt machines, she walks by them and heads to the toppings section.

"Aisha, aren't you getting yogurt?" another sweatshirt-wearing student asks.

"Not yet," the girl with the braid says. "I'm going to get cookies on the bottom first. Frozen yogurt is best when made parfait style, with toppings in between layers."

I'm impressed. I never thought of this method before. It makes sense. There will be an even distribution of topping to yogurt. If this Aisha girl represents Finston Prep, these kids are sharp. I wonder what grade she is in.

The line moves up, and Izzy gets her treat first. She doesn't care about following any topping-to-yogurt formula and goes right for the hot chocolate flavor. Izzy's strategy is to fit as many flavors as she can into her cup.

I watch the Finston Prep kids maneuver their way to the toppings section. At the toppings bar, Aisha places crushed cookies on the bottom of her cup. She stops and stares into her pile of smashed-up cookie crumbs. "My nani loves chocolate shortbread cookies, just like these," she says. Her voice wavers. "I don't think she remembers that they are her favorite."

"What do you mean?" another teammate says to Aisha.

Aisha is blinking away tears. "Mom says she has Alzheimer's disease. She has memory loss and didn't know who I was when I saw her yesterday."

Aisha's teammate gives her a hug. "I'm so sorry."

Aisha wipes at her eyes. "I just don't want this to distract me from QuizBowl. I want to give it my all this year. It's my last one until the high school team."

It's my turn to step up to the yogurt machines. I leave the two of them in this private moment. Without talking to me, Aisha gave great tips on making the best frozen yogurt. She also shared valuable information about herself as well. I got my answer about what grade she's in.

I resist the urge to layer using Aisha's tips. I don't want them to know I was listening in on their conversation. I also feel a little jealous I didn't think of the idea myself.

When I get back to the table the Kagan team is busy eating. Derek leans forward. His sleeve is touching the top of his yogurt. "Did you find out anything interesting?" he says.

I bite down on a spoonful of cold, tart yogurt. One of the boba balls pops, sending a burst of strawberry into my mouth. "Yup."

Izzy leans back in her chair and whistles. "Of all places, they have a meetup here."

I look at my friend. "Are you thinking what I'm thinking?"

Her eyes sparkle. "I think so."

"On the count of three, you say what your thoughts are, and I'll say mine."

Izzy nods. "Got it."

I hold out my fingers for a countdown. "One... two... three..."

"Practice match!" I yell.

"Food fight!" Izzy screams at the same time.

I throw up my hands. "We aren't having a food fight at FroGo! Steven won't give us the discount if we trash the place."

"Oh yeah." Izzy sounds disappointed. "I for sure wasn't thinking a practice match."

I look around at our table. "What do you all say?" I ask. "Finston Prep's team is also here. We can have a practice throwdown, right here at FroGo."

Derek is spooning the last of his yogurt into his mouth. "Why?"

I sigh loudly. It's time to make an executive decision. "It will be good to see what they're like."

No one really reacts. "Okay!" I say. "I guess that means it's a yes?"

Izzy looks at me and then at the team. I know she's trying to be supportive, but I'm sure she's thinking I'm nuts. "We'll do it," she says with some amount of confidence.

Everyone else nods. Full of hope, I walk up to Steven. "Hey," I say, tapping my brother on the back. "Can we have a QuizBowl practice round here?"

Steven wipes down an empty table. The store has started to clear out and there aren't as many customers. He shakes his head and lets out a laugh. "You have certainly made my work shift more interesting today. Thanks for the big tip, by the way."

"Thank Mom," I say. "So, what do you think?"

He looks around the store and shrugs. "Why not? We just hit the dead hour. There isn't as much traffic."

"Can you be the moderator for us?" I ask. "You read us the questions?"

My brother holds his hands out. "Hey, now. I didn't say I wanted to participate in your middle school activity."

"I'll make you cookies this week. Salted chocolate chip."

Steven doesn't seem motivated.

"Fine," I say. "Cookies *and* a three-layer chocolate cake."

He pauses. "Make it malt flavor with that chocolate drizzle you do. I'll throw in free yogurt coupons for the winner. I got a date with Quinn coming up. and it's her birthday next week."

I nod. My brother's girlfriend does like my baking. "You got it."

Motivated by Steven's desire to help me out, I walk over to the Finston Prep kids. I take a deep breath.

"Hi," I say. I lean a hand on their table. "I'm Leah. Captain of the Kagan Middle School

QuizBowl Team. I noticed you all are from Finston Prep. We go against you soon."

The other team looks unimpressed. Maybe because we don't have sweatshirts yet. *Note to self: Get team sweatshirts.*

Aisha sits up straight. "What of it?"

Gone is the heartbroken girl feeling sad about her grandmother's health. She's got her game face on. She looks as if she's daring me to step up. I smile back. Challenge accepted.

I toss my hair over my shoulder. "We wanted to see if you're up for a practice round."

I hold out the coupons Steven gave me. "Winner takes free yogurt. The coupons are good till next year. What do you say?"

The Finston Prep kids look at each other. They glance at the coupons. Back at Aisha. I notice a bright yellow TEAM CAPTAIN button on her sweatshirt. I make a mental note to order a captain button for myself, too.

Aisha stands up and holds her hand out. I take it. "It's a deal."

FroGo Café is thrown into commotion as tables are pushed together to make a makeshift competition area. Soon, in the back of the yogurt shop, there are two rows of tables. Each team sits at the tables, lined up like a QuizBowl game-day match. Instead of buzzers, we each have a plastic spoon and an empty yogurt cup in front of us. To "buzz in" we have to drum or slam our spoon onto the upside-down yogurt container.

Steven stands at the front of the tables with my phone out. He quickly studies the rules. One of his coworkers will act as the "buzzer"—or spoon—keeper.

"Welcome to this first annual FroGo QuizBowl," Steven says. "We will start with a toss-up question, where any team can chime in. It will be worth fifteen points. If the question is not answered right, it will go to the other team."

I smile. Work must be really boring right now for my brother to get so into this.

Steven's coworkers cheer. "Go, QuizBowl!" they say.

"Finston Prep. Kagan Middle," Steven calls out. "First question. 'The old Taylor can't come to the phone right now' is a lyric in what 2017 song by what artist?'"

I forget how to speak. This is a pop-music question, and it throws me completely off.

Someone from Finston Prep hits a spoon. "Taylor Swift!" he yells. "I mean, the song is 'Look What You Made Me Do,' but the artist is Taylor Swift."

"Correct!" Steven yells. "Fifteen points to Finston Prep." Finston Prep jumps up and down, all alike in their matching sweatshirts. They celebrate like they are at a Taylor Swift concert, not in the middle of a neighborhood frozen yogurt shop. Taking the first question is a good confidence booster. A strategy I was hoping to have.

I'm stunned. We've been so entrenched in learning history, science, and politics, we haven't touched on modern culture. The rest of the Kagan team looks shocked as well.

"Next question!" Steven shouts, clearly into his role as moderator. "For ten points. The ruins of the Colosseum and Circus Maximus are found in what modern-day city, also known as an ancient empire?"

Izzy gets to the spoon buzzer first. "Rome," she says.

Steven pumps a fist in the air. "Correct!"

We battle like this for twenty minutes, going through questions at lightning speed. Kagan manages to get ahead by a question, but not enough to have a clear lead.

"For fifteen points," Steven says. "Name the character. This furry blue individual, also featured in a children's television show that premiered in 1969, realizes he is, in fact, the monster at the end of this story."

I slam my spoon down, but I'm a second late. Finston Prep has already gotten control of the answer. Aisha is given permission to speak first.

She casually glances my way, and our eyes meet. "Grover," she says. There's a hint of smugness in her voice. Something about her reminds me of Moira, of feeling like I'm the new girl who'll never truly fit in. A competitive streak boils up inside me.

Suddenly we are in the final round. "Last question, for the win," Steven says. He pauses dramatically. Even the frozen yogurt customers not participating in QuizBowl are hanging on his every word. Everyone at FroGo is watching our practice. "For another ten points," Steven continues, "what is the name of the book, and who is the author?"

This time, I'm the first one to throw my spoon down.

"Kagan," Steven says, and points to me.

"The Monster at the End of This Book," I say. Even though we didn't study pop culture, I remember this book from when I was younger. Suddenly I realize I don't know the author. Even if I got the first part of the question right, I'll lose out on all points if I can't remember the answer to the last section. "Sesame Street?" I throw out the only thing I can think of.

Steven makes an exaggerated sad face, a look of mock pity. "I'm sorry, no. Incorrect!"

He had a bit too much fun shouting that at me.

Steven turns toward the other team. "Finston Prep for the steal?"

Their team huddles together. They have thirty seconds to consult with each other. After a quick discussion, Aisha straightens up from the group. Again, she looks right at me. This girl is fierce.

"The Monster at the End of This Book," she says. Taking a page from my playbook, she

doesn't break eye contact. "By Jon Stone."

Steven winds his arms around like a pinwheel. "Correct! Finston Prep for the win!"

Finston Prep cheers and they all hug one another. Like a good sport, I set an example for my team and clap in congratulation. Inside, I'm fuming. I'm determined to kick their butts the next time. There's going to be only one team that is a QuizBowl champion. It's going to be Kagan.

8.

I continue to keep anything about QuizBowl away from my parents. They still think I'm in art club. Instead, I'm leading team practices on Tuesdays in Ms. Levari's room. We study hard—this time learning *all* the categories and not disregarding pop culture. That was my mistake, and I'm determined to make up for it. Before we left FroGo last Saturday, we challenged Finston Prep to another rematch, the week before our actual match. They accept, and we meet them at FroGo on another Saturday afternoon.

This afternoon, we are missing Luke. He had

soccer and couldn't make it. Not having him there makes Izzy a little grumpy. I don't care as much. With sports, he isn't available like everyone else. With the number of practices Luke has missed, he's the team member who knows the least. While we rotate the role of alternate, this position will most definitely go to Luke. Him not being here for the rematch today makes Izzy also not want to be here, or at least practice QuizBowl questions.

She tells me so in person when we meet at the yogurt shop. "Leah," she says, pulling me aside from everyone else. "What if we hang out with the Finston Prep kids and just chill, not have a rematch? Look at us. We're all burned out."

She gestures toward the team. Their shoulders are slumped, and Derek rubs his eyes after a big yawn.

"It's been a long week, I know," I say. "But we have to focus. We'll get more energy once everything gets going."

I have never been so wrong. We are ten minutes in, about halfway through, and Finston Prep takes the lead in the majority of the answers. We get to the "buzzer" just moments behind. There's no way we can be this slow. Maybe Steven is giving Finston Prep an advantage. Whatever is going on, it's depressing. Luckily, our losing streak is broken when Izzy saves us by answering a correct question about the branches of the United States government.

During break time, each team hangs out at their own table. The FroGo employees give each team a few pieces of candy. Maybe the sugar will help give the Kagan team some energy, because we look defeated.

"Why did we do this?" Derek complains. He chews on a Skittle. "After they kick our butts today, they'll be even more sure of themselves when they see us next week. We need to do something to get back in the game."

Izzy crosses her arms. "This team is really snobby. Stupid matching sweatshirts."

She looks at me. "Are we going to get something like that?"

"I don't think so," I say. "Ms. Levari doesn't think we have enough funding. We can all wear the same color shirt, though."

Derek has got a point. I need to do something to turn this game around. I'm not sure if a pep talk will be the right motivation. Maybe I need a distraction. I look around the room for inspiration. When my gaze falls on the topping bar, I spot the crumbled cookies. An idea forms.

I clap Derek on the back. "Don't worry," I say. "We got this."

After helping a customer check out, Steven calls us back to our tables. He is taking the role of moderator very seriously.

"That's it?" Derek says to me as we get back into our positions. "That was your motivational speech?"

I flip my empty cup upside down again, ready to pounce when needed. "Trust me," I say. "I know what I'm doing."

The break is over and both teams line up at our tables. Finston Prep looks as confident as before. Not Kagan Middle. Our assurance is wavering.

Steven welcomes us back to the second and final round of this FroGo QuizBowl practice. "First question in round two," he says. "For ten points. The Spanish name of this animal, which was first sighted in Puerto Rico, is 'goat sucker' for the way it drinks the blood of—"

I throw down a spoon before Steven finishes the question. He looks at me in surprise. "Kagan?"

I don't say anything. A couple of seconds go by. I make a big show of trying hard to remember the answer.

"Shoot," I say. "It was on the tip of my tongue, but I forgot!"

Now it's my turn not to lose eye contact with Aisha. "I'm losing my mind." I let out a carefree laugh. "It's like I'm some little old lady with dementia."

My words hang heavy in the air.

"No," Steven says. "I'm sorry, Kagan, that is incorrect."

He turns to the other team. "Finston Prep for the steal?"

All of Aisha's self-confidence is gone. Her mouth is open; her lower lip trembles. She stands up. Aisha grabs her bookbag and rushes out the FroGo Café front door.

Her friend looks at me with suspicion. "Creep," she says.

She quickly follows Aisha outside. The rest of their team looks confused.

Steven calls us to attention. "Is she coming back?" he asks Finston Prep.

They shrug and whisper to one another.

Steven holds his hands up. "All right, then. You only have three players, so an incomplete team. For some unknown reason, it looks like Finston Prep is forfeiting the practice match."

He turns to us. "This means that Kagan Middle, you take the win."

Our team looks just as baffled, but then happy. We hug one another and cheer.

The remaining Finston Prep kids collect their things and leave the building. Steven hands the yogurt coupons to my team. The winners.

Our QuizBowl team has no idea what has just happened, but they don't care. They are cheering and fist-bumping each other. Derek goes up to the counter to claim his free yogurt immediately.

Izzy is giving me a strange look. "Way to go, Kagan!" I say. Relief floods my voice. I was a good leader and got morale up. Everyone seems happier. As a bonus win, we now have extra yogurt.

I straighten my back and go to cash in my free yogurt too. I head to the toppings first. Placing cut strawberries on the bottom, I make my next yogurt like a parfait. Layers of strawberry and boba sit between swirls of yogurt.

My first bite is cold, and the taste of Sour Patch Kids hits me in the back of my throat—sweet and salty, but good. I take another spoonful and savor this second bite. I know I'm meant to be captain. I'll do whatever it takes to win QuizBowl.

9.

The lunch bell rings. Like usual, I go to the secret locker room to meet the rest of Team Awkward. With Veterans Day yesterday, we had a day off. Today is Tuesday, the first day of school this week. I sit next to Jojo on one of the benches. She's arguing with Ryan about giving Lovebug a haircut.

"I think a lion cut would be so cute," Ryan says. "He's already so fluffy. Lovebug has the perfect fur. Think of how awesome he'd look with a mane."

Jojo throws a cucumber slice at her. "He's not the right kind of cat," she says. "Savannah cats are short-haired. That kind of cut isn't possible."

Ryan picks the cucumber off her shirt and tosses it in the ziplock bag in her lunch bag. We have a rule not to leave any garbage in our secret locker room. We don't know if anyone else comes here, including custodians. So we take our trash with us and throw it out somewhere else.

"Aw," Ryan says, "you know what kind of cat Lovebug is. You're invested in learning about him. I knew you were a cat lover underneath all that grumpiness."

Jojo gives Ryan a bewildered look. "What else am I supposed to talk to Paul about? Cats are an easy subject. It's all Mr. Meow knows about."

Paul, or Mr. Meow, the social media cat-fluencer, is Jojo's mom's boyfriend. He produces cat content on social media and gifted everyone in Team Awkward *Anything is pawsible!* Mr. Meow notebooks and stickers. Ryan hung one of his posters on the locker room wall.

Izzy comes into the room. There's another spot next to me on the bench. She sees the available seat and pauses. She sits down on another bench instead.

Ryan doesn't notice the snub. She offers Izzy some of her lunch.

I pull my own food out and join in the conversation, trying to ignore the fact that Izzy is avoiding looking directly at me. "Face it, Jojo," I say. "Mr. Meow, and cats, aren't as bad as you thought. Did you know that cats have two hundred thirty bones? More than humans!"

Izzy sighs loudly. "Can we leave the QuizBowl facts out of Team Awkward? We all know you're a walking internet search of information."

My hands stay frozen on my bento box. "That was something I read in our study packet," I explain. "It wasn't like I went searching for information on my own."

Jojo shrugs, clearly missing any tension in the room. She swipes one of my shortbread cookies. I would have stolen one of these too. I've dipped them in milk chocolate and sprinkled them with sea salt.

"Do you want one?" I say to Ryan but not Izzy.

Ryan smiles and takes a treat.

Jojo bites into the cookie. "As long as Paul's cats keep out of my room and away from chewing holes in my clothes," she says, "we are good."

"I brought homemade hummus," Ryan says to Izzy. Ryan holds out a plastic container filled with crackers and whipped dip. "Want some? I made it this morning and drizzled a little pesto on top."

"These are rice crackers?"

"Yes," Ryan says.

Izzy selects one and dips it in the hummus. "Thanks," she says and takes a bite. "This is delicious! Even better than cookies."

Ryan doesn't notice the dig at me and blushes. "I'm glad you like it. You weren't so happy with the cauliflower cream cheese spread I made last time."

Izzy makes a face. "Yeah, because cauliflower." She quickly glances in my direction. "Although I'd take any vegetable over frozen yogurt."

I bristle. "What's wrong with frozen yogurt?" My voice sounds hard, like I've sharpened it with steel.

Jojo appears puzzled. "Who would eat cauliflower over frozen yogurt?"

"After what happened at FroGo," Izzy says, "I don't want to eat that stuff ever again."

"Why not?" I say. "You seemed to enjoy the

chocolate yogurt you had at a *discount* during QuizBowl practice."

"You're right," she says. "Maybe *I'm* not the one who should cut back on the frozen yogurt." Izzy holds my gaze and dips another cracker into the hummus. "Maybe it's you."

I flip open my bento box and pull out an apple slice. Izzy and I are locked in a staring contest. "Why," I say, then take a loud bite of the apple slice, "do you think this?"

Izzy raises her eyebrows. "The desire to win free yogurt seems to have frozen over your already-cold heart."

We eat a couple more bites of our lunch in silence and glare at each other. Jojo and Ryan exchange glances.

Ryan slowly crunches down on her cracker. "So, um . . . everything okay between you two?"

I finish my apple slice and pull out another. "Yeah, Izzy," I say, before sinking my teeth into the fruit. "Is there something you want to say to me?"

Izzy is clutching her lunch box tight. "I know you overheard that Finston Prep girl talking about her grandmother. That was really cruel to throw it in her face like that, Leah."

I stick my chin out. "It's not my fault she's so sensitive."

Izzy looks like she wants to hurl her lunch at me. "*Sensitive?* You used her pain to get her to forfeit the game!"

I'm sitting on the edge of the bench. "How was I supposed to know she would leave? If she was professional, she could have put her feelings aside. Besides, it was just a practice."

"Exactly!" Izzy yells. "That was only a spur-of-the-moment *practice* round for a *middle school* competition. You were shady for absolutely no reason."

It's my turn to hold back from throwing my lunch. Izzy might get her food fight after all. "We absolutely needed that win. If we'd lost, our team would have been afraid going into our real match. I was trying to boost everyone's mood. It worked!"

Ryan is looking at me with horror. "Leah!" she says. "I can't believe you made someone feel bad so you could win. That's . . ." She pauses, as if she's searching for the right word. "Brutal."

I roll my eyes. "It's a *game*. Someone is going to walk away feeling like the loser in this situation no matter what. In every competition, there is a winner *and* a loser."

I turn to Jojo. "Come on, back me up here. You play softball. You know what it's like to be competitive."

Jojo finishes the last of her cucumbers. "Not like that," she says. "Bringing up someone's sick grandma is pretty harsh."

I shove my lunch box into my bag. "You don't know what it's like to want something so bad that others don't care about. You're just like my parents. They didn't want me to do QuizBowl. I thought you'd understand."

Izzy doesn't look moved. "Leah, this is more than just wanting something. You're being too intense about QuizBowl. Maybe you shouldn't have started lying about it in the first place."

I stand up. "Oh look, I hear the bell. I'll see you all later."

I collect my things and remove the book propping the door open. When I leave, I slam the door of the secret locker room behind me.

10.

I poke at the cheese soufflé, watching the eggy sides jiggle.

"Everything all right, Leah?" Mom asks as she takes a bite of her food. She's eating a piece of candied bacon. This family recipe of bacon covered in brown sugar is delicious and indulgent.

I can't help but feel annoyed. Mom makes everything whimsical and carefree. Breakfast for dinner. Sugar on bacon. She has no sense of boundaries, even when it comes to feeding the family. It's a regular Tuesday night. There is school tomorrow and nothing special about today for Mom to make this dish. I realize she is waiting for me to respond.

"I'm fine." I take a sip from my glass. There's an unexpected tartness in the drink. I meet Mom's eyes. "Is there something going on with this orange juice?"

Mom smiles and holds out her own glass, like she's going to make a speech. "I put in some grapefruit juice. I think it adds a little zing."

Dad thumps the table and holds his glass up as well. "Delightful," he says. "Cheers!"

Across the table, Steven joins the toast. "Hear, hear!"

They are so corny. I feel all eyes on me. I know they expect me to also be a part of this spontaneous celebration.

Not today. For once I would like to have a typical, normal meal. With no clinking of glasses or breakfast for dinner just because everything needs to be different or have some sort of creative spin to it. I push the glass away. In this house, even the juice is extra.

I slide my seat out, the chair legs screeching against the hardwood floor. "I'll just have some water, thank you."

I go to grab a new glass from the cupboard. There are no clean ones, so I reach for a mug. My hand wraps around one with a ceramic basketball hoop on the rim. I take inventory of our dishes. None of them match.

Our plates are all in different patterns, purchased from thrift stores. The drinkware is the same. We have souvenir glasses from theme parks we've never been to. To my parents, they are kitschy and fun. Just like the paint-by-number art that hangs on our walls. Picked up from thrift stores as well, a donation from people we do not know.

I'm being a bit dramatic, but I feel suffocated by all this chaos. Why can't we have white plates of similar size and shape? Is it too much to want some form of structure? I pour myself water and try to push away the urge to run out of the kitchen and hole myself away in my room. I already stormed out of the secret room today after my fight with Izzy. It didn't make me feel any better. I don't know if sneaking away from dinner will do me any good.

When I get back to the table, Mom and Dad

are talking to Steven. I eat my breakfast dinner, which now has gone a little cold. I don't really hear their conversation because a replay of the blowup with Izzy is too loud in my head. She was so mad at me.

Izzy and I usually have a good understanding. She and I aren't sporty like Jojo. Or artistic like Ryan. We're kind of the middle-of-the-group people. She's in her sister's shadow, and I'm constantly trying to define myself outside my family. Now, though, Izzy and I are on opposite sides. She's barely talking to me. She didn't even come to QuizBowl after school today.

Worst of all, Izzy hasn't answered any of my QuizBowl questions in our group text. She's usually the first one to chime in. Now she's gone quiet. This silent treatment stinks.

I hear Dad calling my name. "Leah?"

I blink fast. "Yeah?"

Dad and Mom exchange glances. Dad wipes his mouth with a napkin.

"I'll start with the High and Low today," he says with a smile. "We'll go around the table. Steven, you're after me."

"High and Low" is family dinner tradition. By Miller family law, everyone is required to say what our best part of the day was (the High) and the worst (the Low). We can say two Highs, but never two Lows. Ever the optimist, Dad has made a rule that we can always find something good to say about our day. If we've had a particularly hard day, he says finding the light in the darkness makes the glow more worth it. I think Dad sometimes wishes he were a writer instead of a dentist.

Dad pops a blueberry into his mouth. "My High is this dinner. From the soufflé to the bacon, the waffles, and the fruit salad, it's perfection."

My brother throws his head back so his hair gets tossed around his face. He looks up at the ceiling. Finally, he is also annoyed at my parents. He's on my side now.

"Dad," Steven says, "that's such a cheap answer. You always use dinner as a High."

Dad nods, his face serious. "It usually is. Especially this one. It feels wrong to have breakfast this late, which makes it feel oh so right."

Mom laughs. She looks pleased that Dad appreciates her efforts at creativity in the kitchen.

"My Low is that we had a couple of no-shows at the office today," Dad continues. "That's always a bummer. I miss seeing my patients."

Steven raises his hand. "My turn."

Mom is pouring herself another glass of juice. "Go for it."

"My Low is that I forgot to bring lunch to school," Steven says. He glances in my direction and beams. "My High is that thanks to Leah and friends, I had extra tip money and got myself a burrito."

I'm mid-bite, with a piece of fruit dangling on the edge of my fork. I hurry and chew. Steven and his big mouth. By mentioning my friends at FroGo, he's practically on the verge of spilling my QuizBowl secret. My mouth suddenly feels dry. I gulp down the water in my mug. Still thirsty, I grab the glass of juice.

"That's my High too," I say quickly. "Steven."

My brother looks taken aback, and pleasantly shocked. "I don't remember the last time I was my little sister's High."

I give Steven one of my best fake plastic smiles. "There's a new flavor at FroGo Café and he let me have some samples."

I rub my stomach. "The mango passionfruit was so good."

I can feel the sweat start to bead on my forehead. Why did I involve my brother in this scheme? Steven wouldn't purposely sabotage me, but he's absent-minded. He could ruin this. After I made him a chocolate malt cake for Quinn's birthday, too.

Mom looks at me with curiosity. "I didn't realize you were going to Steven's store so much."

"Yeah," I say. "It's just across the street from the school. There's always time for frozen yogurt."

I drain the glass of grapefruit mixed with orange juice. Thinking about the juice, I realize it's actually slightly sweet. I pour myself another glass.

Mom and Dad are studying me. I wonder if they are trying to figure out why I suddenly like this mixed-up orange juice that I pushed away just minutes ago. Or do they think there is something else going on?

As the guilt creeps over me, I know I'm about four questions away from telling them everything. If the conversation starts to drift toward art club, I'm going to crack.

I decide to change the subject by telling Mom and Dad an actual truth—something I usually try to avoid.

I look down at my plate. "My Low is that I got into a fight with a friend today," I say. "It wasn't physical, like we threw punches or anything. But her words still hurt."

This honesty feels raw. Like I'm opening something up I didn't know I needed to share. My fight with Izzy *has* left me spinning. I hate how I left the secret locker room before lunch was even over. That is supposed to be the Team Awkward safe space. It's a room where we come together, not push one another away.

Something dawns on me. Saying my Low out loud helps me realize why I am so grumpy. I'm not really all that bugged by Mom and her breakfast for dinner. I'm upset at what happened between Izzy and me. Having a falling-out with a new friend, at a new school . . . it almost feels like my entire social life is hanging in the balance.

Mom is chewing slowly. I can tell she's fluttering between wanting to pry and wanting to respect my boundaries.

"I'm sorry, Leah," she finally says. Mom has her body turned to face only me. "Do you want to talk about it?"

I stab at my soufflé and watch it deflate into a mushy pile of pale yellow custard. "I'm just more passionate about a project at school than one of my friends," I explain. "She doesn't understand why it's so important. She thinks I'm being too intense."

Although this description of my QuizBowl fight with Izzy is vague, I'm surprised I've even said this much. I'm trying to keep this after-school club hidden from my parents, but now I'm revealing other things I wouldn't normally share.

Dad looks thoughtful. "It's good to recognize that you feel strongly about things," he says. "If it's important to you, maybe talk to your friend. I know you're important to her."

Izzy and I haven't known each other very long. We are new friends at Kagan Middle. Yet Dad's right. I know I'm important to her because she's important to me.

I feel a little lighter at his advice. Maybe if Izzy understood how significant QuizBowl is, she might feel differently about my tactics. While we're becoming close, we don't know each other all that well. If she knew about my kooky family, she might see why QuizBowl is something that is all mine, and how I need to win.

"Thanks, Dad," I say. "I might do that."

When dinner is over, Steven takes my plate to the sink. I think this is his way of apologizing for bringing up my trip to FroGo. He also helps me clear the rest of the table without being asked. I wonder if my opening up about Izzy has him feeling sorry for me. When he gives me a quick one-armed side hug, I know it's not pity. It's compassion. I let my family in. They feel closer to me.

For a moment I feel a brief glow in my chest, knowing how much my family cares about me. Then I remember that I'm also hiding something from Mom and Dad, and the moment of closeness shrinks.

"Hey, Leah," Mom calls from the kitchen. "I'm done washing. Come help me dry the dishes."

I place the bottle of maple syrup in the fridge and walk over to the kitchen sink. Mom hands me a dish towel.

"So," Mom says, handing me a clean, wet plate. "What are you working on in art club right now?"

The plate slips in my hands, and I almost drop it. I try to act natural and remember I've been preparing for this scenario. I knew Mom would ask me about art club. It's why I've been studying art on my own, or at least reading up on it. I've missed so many sessions now.

"This week, the club is learning printmaking," I say. This is what I remember from the syllabus. I place the plate on a dish rack.

Mom hands me a clean glass. "Oh, like screen-printing T-shirts?" she asks. "I remember making some of those in college. We'd sell shirts for our band."

"No," I answer. "We are doing linocuts and then printing them on paper. Although I think you can also print on other materials, like canvas bags." I pick up another dish. "The assignment is to carve out an image on a linoleum sheet block," I continue, like I'm an expert. "We use all these sharp tools to make fine lines to scoop the shape out of the linoleum."

"Sounds fun," Mom says. "What are you doing on your block?"

She doesn't know this, but I've done absolutely nothing on it. I need to make something up. Fast.

"A tree," I blurt out. I take another plate from her. Everything in art is a tree to me.

"It's kind of blobby in shape, but has lots of leaves and branches," I explain. I'm picturing the perfect tree, full of symmetry and shape, with branches stretching across the page. "It's the best one in the group."

I don't know why I add that last part, but it feels like it could be true. If I were to carve a tree on a linoleum block, I would want to mine to shine above the rest. If I actually tried to be an artist, I think I could be a good one.

Mom places her dish sponge down. She rests gloved hands on the edge of the sink and turns toward me. "Leah, that is a disappointing attitude. This time in art club is not about comparison. What makes art special is how others feel when they see your creation, and what it means to you."

Mom's words sting. I was just soaring above the clouds, having a make-believe moment about being the creative child she's always wanted. For a few moments, I could see myself as an artist. My mother has a way of deflating any air in my sails.

"Okay, yeah, Mom, *sure*," I say.

I take a few plates and place them in the cupboard. "Isn't it nice, though, that *some* people, even if it is the art club teacher or students, are proud of what I'm doing?"

Why can't Mom be happy with who I am? I like competition and doing well. I find more fun in science than fantasy. Mom is always trying to change me to make me more like her.

I can't be around Mom right now. I dry the last of the dishes and place the damp dish towel on the counter. "I'm going to go help Steven put the rest of the food away."

As I place the leftovers in storage containers, a sense of defiance crawls over me. It's not like I'm doing anything terrible. My grades are good. I'm home on time. I clean my room. I'm here right now, putting away the food like I'm supposed to. Wouldn't most parents give anything to have a kid who is this well-behaved? I remember overhearing a conversation my parents had about parent-teacher conferences. Mom joked that she wished these meetings with my teachers were more exciting. Just once, she wanted to hear about why I got sent to the principal's office or had after-school detention.

I shove the last strips of bacon into the container and force the lid down. I've never been disobedient about anything in my life. And now that I am, I'm only hiding the truth about QuizBowl. Something about it, though, feels like a little more. By doing QuizBowl instead of art club, I'm participating in something because it's what *I* choose to do.

Not what my parents, my teachers, or any other adult has in mind for me.

I feel terrible for hiding things from Mom and Dad. At the same time, it feels good, in a different way. Like I am being something I didn't think I was. And that feels liberating.

I place the bacon in the fridge. After we win the first tournament, I know I'll feel even better.

11.

My alarm goes off at six thirty, but I've been awake since five a.m. Avery is sitting on the foot of my bed. Noticing I'm awake, she stretches, showing off her long body. She starts to knead at a knitted blanket.

I sit straight up. "Avery, you'll snag it!" I say to her. I shoo her away with my hand.

Avery looks bugged that I even noticed. I don't think she likes it when I occupy her early daylight hours with my tossing and turning. Although, right up until now, I've been lying completely still, staring at the glow-in-the-dark stars on my ceiling.

Over the course of the night, they've lost their light and are now just plastic shapes.

I do my own stretching and put my feet on the floor. This is the second time this week I haven't been able to sleep.

Sometimes, my anxiety will wake me up early. I read that it's best not to lie in bed when this happens. If I'm up and I can't get back to sleep after twenty minutes, I'll make sure to get out of bed. This way, I'm out of my head and on my feet.

But Mom and Dad told me that even if my nerves get the best of me and I can't go back to sleep, I shouldn't go downstairs. They don't want me on my cell phone or watching TV. They also don't want me doing any midnight baking.

So I spend time in my bedroom. Arrange the school supplies on my desk. Study for a test. Write in my journal. Color-code my sock drawer. Tidy up the room.

These bouts of insomnia don't happen all the time, but they happen enough that I'm familiar with this process. I'll wake up with my mind racing about something coming up. Sometimes I'll worry that I forgot to read over my essay for English. Or

I need to study for the math quiz. Once I fretted so bad about whether Steven had eaten all the honey ham, I couldn't stand not knowing if he'd saved me anything, so I broke my parents' rule and snuck downstairs. I wanted to check the fridge and make sure there was enough ham for my lunch. There was. Since I was already up, I made Steven a sandwich too.

This morning, my mind is racing about Quiz-Bowl. Our first meet is this weekend. Against Finston Prep. With Aisha, the girl with the sick grandmother. Thinking about her, I feel conflicted. What I did maybe wasn't exactly fair, but Aisha seemed kind of snotty. Maybe she needed to be taken down a notch. I just don't know if it was my place to do it.

Having members of my team like Izzy know about my questionable tactics only makes me feel worse. We won the match by forfeit, and for a few moments the team seemed better. I just wish I didn't feel like a dark cloud was constantly following me around.

Is the Kagan Middle School team ready for our upcoming match? Am I being the best team captain? Should I have given Derek a shot at team captain since he is older? I wonder if it was a little wrong to take this leadership aspect of QuizBowl away from him since I still have two more years at the school.

Maybe I'm taking over the team too much. I went to bed with worry gnawing at my heart. It has stayed there, slowing eating me up.

It's now late enough that it's not weird that I'm up. I hurry and get ready for the day. I head downstairs, straight to my cell phone, which has been charging in the kitchen. It's time to send out my daily motivational QuizBowl text. Since we're so close to the match, I'll throw in a baking incentive today. I text the group:

For ten points—or a bag of Nutella Chocolate Sandwich Cookies that I'll bring to school—name these segmented animals of the phylum Annelida that help aerate plant roots as they burrow through the soil.

I place my phone down and get out a bowl for cereal. I know I won't get responses right away. Most everyone will also be getting ready for school. Our team is using the honor system not to do an internet search for the answer.

As I munch on honey oat flakes in almond milk, I remember I did get a couple of likes on yesterday's QuizBowl question by 7:10 a.m. And someone chimed in with the correct answer at 7:15 a.m.

I look out the window at the bright blue sky. It's a new morning, and hopefully a new start. Dad's words about talking to Izzy come back to me. I feel hopeful. He's right. Once she understands why QuizBowl is so crucial to me, she'll be on board with my intensity. Maybe we will be back to sharing lunch again today.

I eat my breakfast in silence. Rinse my bowl and load it into the dishwasher. Put everything back and start to pack my lunch. In the pantry, I can't find the box of granola bars I like.

I look at my phone. 7:20 a.m. Not a single acknowledgment from my team. No one has bothered guessing the answer. It's ten minutes past the time I got a response yesterday. Am I slipping up as a leader? I feel the familiar hold of anxiety chewing at my chest.

"Has anyone seen the granola bars?" I yell from the kitchen. "The ones with the chocolate and peanut butter chips?"

Steven enters the kitchen and sits down at the table. His hair is a mess, and he hasn't put his contacts in yet. He's still wearing his glasses. "Oh, those ones?" he yawns. "I know why you like them. They're good. I ate the last one yesterday." Steven pours himself some cereal. "We need to tell Mom to get more."

"You ate *all* the granola bars?"

Steven takes a bite of his breakfast and points his spoon at me. "Just because I ate the *last* one doesn't mean I finished the entire box."

I hold my arm out to the pantry. "There's nothing I can take for an after-school snack. You might as well have eaten everything!"

Just then, Mom enters the kitchen. She's already dressed, wearing workout clothes, and holding a mug of tea. "What are you fighting about?"

I wave my hand at Steven. "He took all the granola bars and didn't bother to let anyone know until it was too late."

"It was only one!" Steven yells back.

Just then, the doorbell rings. "Who is coming over this early in the morning?" Steven says.

"Honey!" Mom yells down the hall to Dad. "Will you get the door?"

I'm still glaring at Steven when Ben Walker comes into the kitchen. "Hi, Leah," he says with a wave. "Mr. Jeffers wanted me to give you this package of art supplies. I told him we're neighbors. We haven't seen you in club for a while."

My throat feels dry and it's hard to swallow.

Ben pulls out a blank linoleum sheet and an unopened package of carving tools. *Leah Miller* is scrawled on a piece of scrap paper and clipped to the bag. Ben holds it out in front of him. "Next class we are printing with our blocks. I know you haven't done yours yet."

Ben looks nervously around the kitchen as we all stare at him. "I uh, didn't want you to miss out. I would have given it to you on the bus, but I'm getting a ride from my mom today."

Mom studies the blank lino sheet, which looks as empty as my face right now. "This is your lino project?" she says.

I hurry over to Ben and grab the bag of art supplies. "Thank you," I say. "I must have forgotten this at the last club."

Ben looks puzzled. He zips up his bookbag. "Anyway, maybe I'll see you there."

He leaves, and Dad enters the kitchen after him. Like Steven, his hair is also messed up. He looks confused and alert at the same time. The anxious feelings in my chest are replaced with something else: dread.

Dad tries to rub the sleep out of his eyes. "You haven't been going to art club?" He yawns and stretches, like this conversation is all part of a dream.

I wish it were. It almost feels like this is an out-of-body experience. Having my secret come out like this doesn't feel real. Like it's happening in my subconscious, and I'm trapped, frozen, in a nightmare.

Mom pours herself another cup of tea. She walks over to the kitchen table and pulls out a seat. "What's going on?"

I take a short breath. Maybe this really isn't happening, and I can wake myself up. I pinch my arm. My skin catches on my nail, and I feel a scratch. The hurt is real. This is really happening.

"I may have missed a few times," I say. My voice sounds far away.

Steven places his bowl in the sink. "So, ah. I think I'm just going to go."

As he walks by me, my brother makes one last moment of eye contact. "I didn't eat all the granola bars," he whispers, and rushes out of the room.

Dad sits down next to Mom. He holds his hand out to a chair across from him. "Leah, take a seat."

I slowly lower myself down and sit across from my parents. This is not how I pictured starting my morning. For a small moment, I wonder what my life would be like if I'd chosen art club instead of QuizBowl. Could Ben and I have become friends? Maybe I would have actually liked doing art. It's too late now.

Mom swirls a spoon in her tea. The liquid goes round and round, funneling like a tiny tornado. "What are you doing instead of going to art club?"

"QuizBowl." I gulp. I wish I had some tea to help my dry throat. I'd even take some of that grapefruit-orange juice again.

Mom and Dad both take a deep breath. Mom

looks down into her cup. "Oh, Leah." Her words are hushed. "What are we going to do with you?"

No one says anything for minutes. My parents aren't mad. I know it's early in the morning, but I wish they would at least yell. Stand up, wave their arms, pace around the room.

Instead they just look at me with sad eyes. With disappointment. I would rather have their rage than this pity.

"What are you going to do with me?" My voice cracks. "You can let me go to my QuizBowl tournament this Saturday. And you can come watch."

Dad frowns. "I don't know if supporting your lie is the best way to help."

"I wouldn't have to lie if you would listen to me!" I say. "QuizBowl is important. This is the thing I fought about with my friend. I was trying to tell you how much it meant to me. You only saw what *you* wanted."

I look at my parents. "I feel terrible for lying. I'm sorry. I promise, though, if you come see me compete on Saturday, you'll get an idea of how much this means to me. How much I've put into my team as the captain."

Mom looks alert. "You made captain? As a sixth grader?"

She listened to something I said after all.

"Yes," I say. "I'm the first sixth grader at Kagan Middle to be captain. I didn't even think I had a shot since it's my first year at the school. The team has kids from sixth, seventh, and eighth grades. I've been trying really hard to be a good leader. I've arranged for extra after-school QuizBowl practices. We meet at FroGo. It's why Steven brought it up. My friends give him good tips when we go there."

Dad blinks. "Wait, does this mean Steven is in on this too?"

I quickly wave my hands in front of me. "Don't get mad at Steven," I say. "He's actually been a really great brother and has even helped me study." I pause. "Maybe don't let him know I said this. I'll never hear the end of it from him."

Mom and Dad are giving each other the parent glance, where they seem to communicate using some secret look that only they know. Whatever they are saying, it seems to soften their stance on me missing art club.

I decide to be bold. "If my team wins the match

on Saturday, you'll see how it's all been worth it. Please come. We're going crush Finston Prep."

Mom shakes her head. "Leah, we've gone over this. Whether it's recognition for a piece in art club or QuizBowl, it isn't about being the best." She tilts her head to the side and studies me. "Although it sounds like you weren't the best in art club, since you never went. Wow, you really made that convincing."

"I've gone!" I protest.

Dad places a hand on Mom's shoulder. "I think supporting Leah in QuizBowl is something we can do."

Mom drinks the last of her tea. "Okay," she relents. "We'll go to your match. Not because we want to watch you beat the other team, but because we care about you. Win or lose. We will talk about the lying later."

The anxiety is replaced with relief, and it feels like clouds are parting in my chest. Making way for something brighter. I give my parents a quick hug. "Thank you," I say.

I look at the clock in the kitchen. It reads 7:35 a.m. I have five minutes to get out the door and not miss my bus. After a quick scramble to collect my things, I'm soon sitting on the school bus on the way to Kagan Middle School.

In the pocket of my sweatshirt, my phone pings. It's 7:43 a.m., and I've finally gotten the first response from the QuizBowl group thread.

Izzy: **earthworms**

I like her response and answer:

Correct. Cookies are yours.

Izzy doesn't respond. All around me buzzes the noise of other kids' conversations. But all I can hear is the silence from my friend and the rest of the QuizBowl team.

12.

It's Saturday, the day of the competition.
I had Mom drop me off a little early so I could have time to think before our match. I hoped Izzy would also be here since we haven't talked much. I haven't had much interaction with the entire team, actually. Part of me wonders if they will even show up.

I push open the auditorium doors of Kagan Middle and the first thing I see is the stage. Two tables are set up around a podium in the middle. Each table has five chairs, each seat representing a place for a member of the QuizBowl team. On the table to the right, there is a banner for our team, the Kagan Cardinals. The other table boasts a sign for the Finston Prep Falcons. For the first QuizBowl match of the year, it's the battle of the birds.

The mascots representing the schools are onstage, doing handsprings and gymnastics stunts to energize the crowd. The PTO went all out. The Kagan cardinal is challenging Finston Prep's falcon to a dance battle. They riff back and forth, copying moves and swaying to the upbeat music coming from the auditorium speakers. The audience loves it. They cheer loudly.

I appreciate how the Kagan community shows up. At this school, everyone is just as enthusiastic for academics as they are for sports. It's a nice balance, and one reason why my parents picked the house we now live in. More important to me than a nice backyard or large bedrooms was to be zoned for a school that was well-rounded. A place that put as much emphasis on the arts and learning as it did on the athletic department. Our school has a philosophy that supportive energy isn't just useful for athletes, but for scholars as well. You can't have a school named after Elena Kagan, a justice of the Supreme Court, and not expect it to value education.

The Kagan cardinal goes to football games and also pumps up the crowds at chess tournaments, orchestra concerts, and today, a QuizBowl showdown. Our mascot is involved in the community as well. He's been to store openings and even appeared in one of Mr. Meow's videos. He pretended to be scared of Paul's cats and tried to fly away. He used a trampoline and did lots of somersaults and tricks. Jojo showed it to us during lunch one day and we all had a good laugh.

Behind me, the Kagan QuizBowl team arrives. I give each of them an encouraging fist bump. As the team captain, I lead the way. I can almost feel the nerves of every single member. They are as real as my own. I know I need to set an example of confidence. I hold my head high as we make our way to the stage.

As we get closer, I spot friends and family in the audience. Jojo and Ryan are there, along with Izzy's sister and parents. Luke, our alternate, sits next to them. My friends cheer enthusiastically when they spot us. They hold up signs that say GO LEAH! GO IZZY! and TEAM AWKWARD ALL THE WAY!

Mom and Dad stand and wave when they see me. They don't hold signs, but they are smiling. Good. When we win, they'll see how all my maneuvering to be on the team was worth it. My parents will be proud of me—in awe of my leadership skills and how I have led the team to victory in our very first match of the season.

Also standing up are the Walkers. My steps slow when I see Ben. He has one hand shoved in his pocket. The other hand he raises in acknowledgment. I return his gesture with a smile, careful not to let it spread all the way across my cheeks. Suddenly, a large foam finger is thrust in front of my face, and I lose sight of Ben.

Steven is in the front row, waving around the foam finger like it's a wand. "Yay, Leah!" he cheers. He points the finger at us, like he's trying to cast a spell. "Touchdown to you, and you, and you!"

I can't help it—I laugh. That's my goofy brother for you.

Unlike me, my brother is actually athletic. Even though I don't play sports, I know enough to tell the difference between football and every other game with a ball. I don't kick anything around for fun, but I do study sports and sports history. I know all about Lionel Messi, the Argentine soccer player who is thought to be one of the greatest players of all time. Japanese American Wat Misaka is considered the first person of color to have played professional basketball. Serena Williams was ranked number one in tennis for over 319 weeks.

I know that pickleball has nothing to do with actual pickles *or* a rumored dog named Pickles. The sport got its name in 1965 from the pickle boat in rowing races. With QuizBowl, questions will come from all sorts of categories, including sports. I may not be a star on the field, but I know enough to hopefully answer correctly.

Our team steps up to the stage. The thrill of seeing Team Awkward, my family, and even Ben, overpowers any nervousness I feel. As we line up at our table, I glance over at Izzy. I had plans to talk to her before the match, but she's kept her distance. There's nothing I can do about our fight now, though. Right now we need to focus.

Onstage, the lights shine down on us. The glare is so bright, we shield our eyes. I see some kids from the journalism club ready to take notes, and there is video recording equipment on the stage. One of the things that makes QuizBowl so unique is that it is streamed on our school social media. Supposedly, having this game in front of a live audience will help us feel important. However, the spotlight can also have the opposite effect on confidence.

As we take our seats, I look around at my team. They all seem a little sick. "Did you all eat something this morning?" I ask. "Hopefully you stuck to foods that are easy to digest, like oatmeal or toast?"

Derek looks at me, his face green. "I had some doughnuts."

I place a hand to my face. "Oh, Derek."

A teacher walks up to us. "Hello, Kagan," she says. "Are you ready for this face-off?"

Izzy brightens when she sees who it is. "Meadow!" she says. "Are you the moderator?"

"Yes, but please call me Ms. Schaeffer for this event," our teacher says with a wink. "I need to dress and sound the part."

I study her outfit. She's right—there is something different about our English teacher. Her usual loose and flowy hair is pulled back. She's also wearing a blazer and a buttoned-up shirt. She looks more put together than she does on a normal day of school.

Ms. Schaeffer leaves us to go talk to Finston Prep. Then she walks over to the podium, and I'm surprised to see that she's even wearing heels.

"Welcome all," she says into the microphone, her voice bright and cheery, "to this QuizBowl matchup between our host school, Kagan Middle, and the visiting opponents, Finston Prep."

She allows the audience a few seconds to clap. The mascots hold hands to their ears—or at least where their ears would be, for birds—as if they want to hear more noise.

Ms. Schaeffer interrupts the cheering. "A reminder of the rules. We kindly ask that the audience members refrain from giving tips or hints. The answers are for the team members only. We have two ten-minute rounds of questions, with a ten-minute break in between. In the event of a tie, the appointed team captains will face off in a bonus round."

She turns away from the spectators toward us on the stage. "Students," Ms. Schaeffer says with a warm smile. "Are you ready?"

Finston Prep looks hyped up. True to form, they have on matching shirts. A different design from the ones they wore to FroGo. All nod at the same time.

I look over at our team. We all are in red, except Derek. His button-up polo looks like it's more of a hot pink. I bite my tongue and don't say anything. We're onstage and seated. The time for changing has already passed.

Ms. Schaeffer again faces the audience. "Participants. Please buzz in and tell us your name, grade, and favorite subject to study in school. Finston Prep, let's have you go first."

Each table is equipped with three microphones and several buzzers Aisha turns one toward her face. Her hair is braided again, this time in a coiled crown around her head. As she introduces herself, she sounds calm and collected. Not at all the emotional girl we saw at FroGo a week ago. She makes even the act of saying her name sound cool.

I can tell why she is the Finston Prep team captain. She has a presence that is commanding, yet it also seems like she can be kind. As I study Aisha, I wonder what I look like to others. Am I a team captain who also cares? Or is my competitiveness the only thing that gets through?

The rest of the Finston Prep team talks. I realize that soon it will be my turn to speak. I try to remember the question and stop thinking about how Aisha did her hair.

What did Ms. Schaeffer ask again? What is my favorite subject at school? At this very moment, I don't know. I didn't prepare for this spontaneous question.

I turn to look at my team. It's as if they can pick up on my hesitancy. Derek starts to wring his hands. He's looking down into his lap. "I can't remember what grade I'm in," he whispers. "Do I say my name or nickname?"

I lean in closer so only the two of us can hear. "What's your nickname?"

"Doobie."

In an attempt to cover up laughter, I start

to cough. I've never heard him called this. A livestreamed QuizBowl tournament isn't the place to introduce it to the world. "Your name is Derek," I say reassuringly. "You're a seventh grader. I know you love robotics." Remembering these things about my teammate helps me regain my confidence. I start to feel excited about the match.

Derek takes a deep breath. "Robotics. That's right." As he remembers pieces of his identity, he seems to chill out.

When it's our team's turn to talk, we all take turns with the microphones. This also serves as a sound check just in case something isn't working. While our team's energy is not high, we at least get through the introductions in one piece.

Ms. Schaeffer holds her arms out.

"We will start with a toss-up question," she explains. "That means anyone from either team can answer. They will receive no help from their team. This question will contain multiple clues to the answer. This first question is worth fifteen points. If not answered correctly, it will go to the other team."

We all sit up straighter. It's time.

"For fifteen points," Ms. Schaeffer says. "The composer Wolfgang Amadeus Mozart wrote a concerto for this instrument. It is a single-reed woodwind instrument tuned to the key of B-flat."

Izzy's hand slams on her buzzer.

Ms. Schaeffer points to her. "Kagan?"

Izzy leans forward into the microphone. "The clarinet."

Ms. Schaeffer nods. "Fifteen points for Kagan."

We got the first question right. This is good momentum.

"Next question," Ms. Schaeffer says. "This substance traps bacteria and dust before they enter the body, preventing anything from entering the lungs."

Someone from Finston Prep beats us to the buzzer.

"Mucus," they say.

"Correct," Ms. Schaeffer chimes in.

For the next few minutes, we fire through questions. Time goes by quickly, and the first round is up. I'm pleased that after an intense ten minutes, we have a slight edge over Finston Prep. Kagan is up five points going into the half. I wish we were further ahead, but this is also acceptable.

From across the stage, I hear a cheer. Looking over at the other team, you would think they are the ones ahead. They high-five one another and look happy.

To be the losers.

I'm baffled. This isn't the way you are supposed to go into the second half if you're behind. I glance over at my teammates, ready to make a remark about Finston Prep, when I see the exact opposite.

The Kagan Cardinals appear tired. Stressed and worried. We're ahead, but the air on our side of the stage feels much more tense. We should be the ones cheering for one another and handing out praise. Instead we mutter to ourselves. Izzy won't even glance in my direction. Everyone else on our QuizBowl team seems miserable.

I avoid looking into the crowd. Do Mom and Dad see how my team is reacting? I don't know what I need to do to help change this attitude, but halftime will be important. In movies about sports, it's always the time where the coach gives some motivational speech that speaks to the heart of everyone in the room. The team leaves the break different. Ready to start anew and kick some butt.

I think about what I can say to increase our faith in ourselves. I wonder if I have it in me to deliver powerful speeches that inspire.

As we stand up to take our break, doubt shadows my confidence. Did I pick the right strategy to win? Maybe I should have been the leader who praises instead of pushes. Whatever kind of captain I am supposed to be, I should figure out a way to cheer my team up.

We need to win.

13.

As we make our way off the stage, the Kagan cardinal is running toward us. Hands in the air, in cheering motion. He is walking up the stairs as we are coming down. As we pass him, the cardinal holds out one of his hands and greets each member of our team with a fist bump. I'm second to last in line, standing at the top of the stairs. I am right behind Derek and followed by Izzy.

Even standing a step below me, Derek is still taller and blocks my view of the cardinal. I feel very small. I wonder if Derek had a growth spurt this week.

As the cardinal makes his way along, I see him tap Derek's fist with his knuckles. When the cardinal approaches me, I hold out my hand, fingers close together. The cardinal misses my outstretched fist. Instead a gloved hand connects with my cheek.

Bam!

Suddenly I am stumbling. There's a gasp from the crowd, and my vision blurs. I was just punched in the face by the Kagan cardinal!

"Leah!" I hear Izzy's voice as I hit the floor. She grabs my arm, keeping me from rolling off the stage.

I'm sprawled out on the floor, just inches from the edge. I blink, and my sight comes into focus. There is a crowd of people around me. One of the faces is Mom. Her face blurs together and multiplies.

"Mom?" I say with some confusion. "Wow, you got over here really fast."

Someone holds my head up. It's Dad. I think I can make out an outline of a person who looks like Ben handing Dad a water bottle. Mom presses the cool metal bottle against my cheek. It takes off some of the sting. I look to my left and see Steven. My brother has his phone out, filming.

"What are you doing?" I say, and try to take a swipe at him. Steven, like my mom, likes to document everything. I'm not sure if I want today's events on a hard drive somewhere, to share with my future children and all future generations.

"I'm just trying to help you be in charge of your own narrative," Steven says.

I hold my head. "Steven, what on earth are you talking about?"

"Listen," he says. "That was so bad what just happened to you. And I'm sure it hurt. But that video is going to be gold. A mascot punching a middle schooler in the face? It doesn't get better than that! It's already caught on camera from other people's point of view. I'm just providing you an up-close-and-personal angle. However you want to show it."

Across the room, Ms. Schaeffer is scolding the mascot. She doesn't keep her voice down, and neither does he.

The Kagan cardinal doesn't remove his mask, but I can hear his muffled voice. "I didn't see her!" the cardinal is saying. "She's short and was standing behind someone much taller. You have no idea how hard it is to see out of this thing."

Part of me feels bad for whoever this mascot is. One thing I know from my study of sports is that mascots are not supposed to speak. Hearing their voice can give away their identity. Whoever just hit me in the face may not be around to cheer at the next QuizBowl game.

Dad helps me to my feet and escorts me off the stage. My head is pounding. When I fell, I also hit my head and landed flat on my back. Good thing it's halftime and I have a few minutes to pick myself up.

We make our way past the Finston Prep team, and some of them look horrified. Most, though, are trying to hold back giggles.

Aisha and her friends stand with arms crossed and lips pursed. As I brush by them, one of her friends whispers, "That's karma for you."

In our team waiting room, which is a classroom down the hall, our advisor, Ms. Levari, hands me an ice pack. "Are you okay, Miss Miller?" she asks. "Does your team need to use the alternate for this next round?"

I press the ice to my face and wave her concern away. "I'm fine," I say. "Just really embarrassed."

Mom and Dad are standing near, ready to act if needed. For once, I appreciate their laid-back approach to parenting. Having Mom and Dad calm is helping me find some composure of my own.

Derek is fiddling with the collar of his shirt. Even if he wore the wrong color, I appreciate his effort. He pulled through and dressed up.

"Maybe we can do a well-check test," Derek says. "You know, ask her things to make sure her brain is working?"

I slowly turn my head. To think I had nice thoughts about Derek and his brave choice of clothing just a moment ago. "Are you kidding me?"

Izzy stands in between us. "Leah's strong," she says. "She'll pass any test." Izzy meets my eye. "What's the capital of Delaware and some of its neighboring states?"

I almost don't answer at first. Is . . . Izzy talking to me?

"Dover," I finally say. "Bordered by New Jersey, Pennsylvania, and Maryland."

Izzy smiles. She is actually smiling at me.

"She checks out fine," she says. She places a hand on my shoulder. "Our captain can take a hit, but she gets back up."

Derek doesn't look convinced. "Let me see about this," he says. "What is the biggest two-digit prime number that is less than one hundred?" He stares me down with something that looks a little bit like a dare.

Derek is throwing a math problem at me. Right now, after I got knocked in the head. Maybe my teammate has more fight in him than I thought. "Ninety-seven."

He looks disappointed. "Yeah, good guess." Derek leans forward, so close I can see his long, strawberry-blond eyelashes. "Who's the best Beatle?"

I place my ice bag down. "That's an opinion. Not a factual question." I pause for a moment. "However, it's Paul."

Derek snorts. He looks at Ms. Levari. "I think Leah might have some brain damage. The answer is definitely John."

Ms. Levari actually appears amused. I manage

to grin as well. The jokes have lightened the mood in the break room and brought out a few chuckles. This is the kind of team spirit we've needed to have all along.

I look at all the adults with us. "Can I have a few minutes alone with the QuizBowl team?"

"Of course," Ms. Levari says as she ushers the adults out of the room. My parents wave goodbye to me, and Steven films himself leaving.

Ms. Levari taps her watch. "You are back onstage in six minutes, so make it fast."

She shuts the door behind her. I face everyone on the team.

"No one wants to get punched in the face," I start. "But if anyone deserved it, it was me."

Izzy shakes her head. "It was an accident. The cardinal couldn't see past Derek's big head."

I feel so happy that Izzy is on my side again. The way she's defending me makes me think I'm forgiven.

"Hey!" Derek says. "I got a haircut yesterday. It's not my fault Leah is too tiny to see."

I let out a laugh. "This wasn't anyone's fault. I don't blame you, Derek." I look at my teammates, who have also become friends. "I think it's almost like . . . karma. At least, that's what I overheard the Finston Prep team say. They are right. I got what I dished out. Except, instead of getting struck with words, I got hit in the face by a large bird."

There is a collective chuckle through the team.

"I'm sorry," I say. It's simple, and I mean it. I realize that the best inspiration is to be honest. With them, and myself. "I got caught up in winning for the wrong reason," I explain. "I've been a terrible tyrant, and I regret it. I'm sorry I've gotten so intense about winning."

Izzy stands next to me. "So, what do you say, Cardinals? Should we go back in there and kick some Falcon butt?"

"Yes!" everyone cheers.

I hold a hand in the air. Hope fills my chest. This humor and self-reflection thing is working. I didn't need an iron fist to lead. I needed to be relatable. "On three," I say, "we all do a big fist bump!"

All the members of our team smile.

"One, two, three!"

Our fists come together in unison.

"Go, Cardinals!"

14.

"Find the least common multiple of the numbers six, eight, and sixteen."

"Forty-eight!"

"Ten points to Finston Prep."

"In computer language, what does the acronym *ROM* stand for?"

"Read-only memory."

"Ten points to Kagan!"

"This autonomous country is the world's biggest island with no connecting roads or railroad system to travel from one community to another."

"Greenland."

"Ten points to Finston Prep."

It's the end of round two, the final round, and the teams are tied. My heart is pounding, and I totally have pit stains. At this point I envisioned us far in the lead, so we wouldn't have to worry about a close contest. Instead it's anyone's game at this point.

In QuizBowl, the team captain is the one to answer the tiebreaking question. Besides leading the overall morale of the team, this tiebreaking is the captain's biggest responsibility. Especially since this is my chance to prove myself to my parents.

I look across at Aisha. Her eyes are determined. Maybe she has the same passion to win this that I do. For a second I can see her stricken face in FroGo again, all crumpled and broken when I said such mean things to throw her game off. Thinking back, I feel ashamed. I don't deserve to win. I wonder if I should just give Aisha the competition. She's been through so much. Would our losing the match be the only way for me to redeem myself to Aisha and her grandmother?

I look down the table to the Kagan Middle

School QuizBowl team. They have worked so hard, and we've come a long way. Gone are the nerves. Everyone looks excited and prepared. We are making jokes and teasing one another. Just the way a real team should behave.

Thinking about those I lead, I know can't sacrifice their win to ease my guilt over Aisha. That's not how games work. At least, not the ones I have studied. I hardly know Aisha and the QuizBowl team at Finston Prep. However, I don't think she would want to win that way.

Ms. Schaeffer looks down at her cards. "Welcome to our bonus round. Captains? Are you ready?"

Aisha and I avoid looking at each other. We both nod. We are prepared for this moment.

Ms. Schaeffer clears her throat. "For the win. This politically driven band from the UK pioneered the 'pay what you want' approach for their 2007 album *In Rainbows*."

Ms. Schaeffer pauses. "Who is the artist that challenged the traditional record-label model of pricing and sparked a discussion about the value of music in the digital age?"

I feel like my heart has jumped into my throat.

I'm not sure if it's the excitement of the last question, or that I know this tiebreaking question is important. I push the buzzer, even though I don't know the answer.

"Kagan?" Ms. Schaeffer says.

I give myself a few more seconds to collect my thoughts. This is a music question. A pop-culture reference that I could memorize fairly easy. For some reason, I know there is a connection to the music my parents listen to. I avoid looking in their direction.

I think of the context clue. It's a band from the United Kingdom that was popular in 2007. In my mind, I comb through Dad's records from this time. Is it Block Party? Muse? I'm sure I've heard it mentioned in our house. Dad likes bands that are disruptive like this.

Who was popular during that time period and from the UK? My time is up. I go with the next band that pops into my head.

"The Arctic Monkeys," I answer.

Ms. Schaeffer is expressionless. "I'm sorry," she says, "that is incorrect. Finston Prep, the question is now yours."

I'm shocked. I should have known the answer! This band is probably somewhere in my DNA. I can almost hear the music floating eerily throughout the room.

Aisha takes a deep breath. "Radiohead," she answers.

As soon as the band name is out of her mouth, I know she's right.

"You are correct," Ms. Schaeffer says. "That tiebreaking question was for the win. This Quiz-Bowl tournament goes to Finston Prep."

An explosion of cheers erupts from the Finston Prep table and all their supporters. Aisha is jumping up and down. She rushes to embrace her teammates.

We didn't win. After all this, we are the losers. I convinced my parents to come to a QuizBowl game so I could show them that I could lead my team to victory. Instead we are leaving in defeat. All because I didn't know Radiohead. I feel like the exact opposite of brilliant right now.

Regardless, the match is over, and I know that I need to put on a brave face. After a few minutes of celebration by Finston Prep and self-reflection by us, I throw on my bookbag and head over to the Finston Prep table. The rest of my team follows my lead.

I walk over to Aisha and hold out my hand. "Congratulations," I say. "The best team won."

I hear the conviction in my voice. Yes, I am saying this to be a good sport. But I realize I also mean it. Finston Prep won fair and square. They, and we, should feel proud of what we did, no matter the outcome.

Aisha studies me for a minute. Then she takes my hand. "Thank you. Your team was a formidable opponent."

She doesn't need to tell me this. But she does, and the compliment feels good. It takes away the sting of losing just a little bit.

"You're kind," I say. "I haven't always been very nice to you."

I reach into my bookbag and take out a plastic container. "I baked something for the Kagan team and made extra," I explain. "I understand if it's weird to eat something made by a stranger. Especially if this person is someone you just beat in QuizBowl."

Aisha nods. "Uh, yeah."

I swallow and go on. "You can throw the cookies away if you want and not eat them," I say. I hand her the container. "I just want you to know that I am sorry for being so awful." I can hardly look her in the face without feeling ashamed.

I force myself to meet her eyes. If I am going to apologize, I need to do it right.

"I shouldn't have used personal information I overheard at FroGo to try and get an advantage in our game," I say.

Getting this apology out of my mouth is harder than I thought it would be. I keep on going.

"I like to bake," I say. "These are chocolate sablé cookies. The recipe is from my favorite baker. Her name is Dorie Greenspan. They are called World Peace Cookies. I hope they bring a little healing for you today."

I've been told I talk at least ten years older than my age. I don't know why I communicate this way, but I can't help it. Right now, though, it's as if I am hearing myself speak out loud for the first time. Ugh. I sound so formal. I keep going.

"I hope you enjoy the cookies," I say. "Or, at

the very least, the thought of them. I know you said your grandmother loved shortbread. These sablés are similar. It's my way of saying sorry. Oh, and the container is reusable."

Aisha takes the cookies. She pops off the lid and takes a chocolate sablé. She holds the container out in my direction so I can also take one.

We both eat the cookies, chewing in silence, but it isn't uncomfortable.

Aisha smiles at me and takes another cookie. "These are delicious," she says. Then she pulls me in for a hug. "Thank you. I can't wait to share these with my nani and tell her all about this. She would love to know how she brought us together."

We let go, and I'm feeling better. I return to my team. This match goes to Finston Prep. They deserved it. But I'm already thinking about a rematch. An informal meetup again at FroGo, or another QuizBowl showdown.

The next time we see them, I know things will be different. We'll have fun, win or lose. And there will definitely be more cookies.

15.

I'm writing in my journal when there is a light tap on the door. Mom opens it. "Care for a late-night banana split?" She holds out two spoons. "Don't worry," she says. "I bought myself some lactose-free ice cream."

I glance at the clock. It's nine thirty p.m. I close my book. "All right," I say, and slide on my slippers. "As long as they aren't Coke floats."

Mom smiles. "We'll save the caffeine for another time."

I follow Mom downstairs. I sit at the kitchen table and watch her assemble the sundaes. She's like an artist. Mom has a way of elevating anything she creates. Even if it's just as simple as scooping out ice cream for a banana split.

I watch her select a colorful bowl, shallow and long. She places a sliced banana first, cut lengthwise. On top of the banana, she places three generous scoops of ice cream.

"Whoa," I say. "I'm not sure if I can eat all that."

Mom doesn't look up. "Of course not. This isn't all for you. We are sharing."

This makes more sense. I continue to watch Mom work. She's a master.

Mom layers homemade hot fudge in a swirly pattern over the mountains of ice cream. Tops each scoop with a blanket of coconut whipped cream, piled high and pillowy. Then comes the showering of chopped nuts and rainbow-colored sprinkles. It's a sight to behold, and I can't wait to dig in.

Mom hands me a spoon. She motions for me to take the first bite. This is ice-cream-sundae perfection. "You know," she says, after taking a large bite, "I was really proud of you today. I heard about your conversation with the Finston Prep girl. You are a good team leader."

I lick whipped cream off my spoon. "No, I'm not. We lost."

Mom shakes her head. "It's not always about being the winner. We've talked about this. Oftentimes when we lose, or fail, this is when we learn the most."

I dig in for another bite of ice cream. "If I was the most learned, I would have gotten Radiohead right." I look at Mom. "Was Dad disappointed that I missed that one, out of all the questions?"

Mom stops to think. "Well . . ."

"Oh my gosh." I'm holding my head in my hands. "I let him down."

"Not at all," Mom says with a smile. "He's just determined now to be a better influence in your music library."

I groan. "Great. Now I'm doomed to hear Dad rock for the next three months."

Mom laughs. "At least!"

We are halfway through the sundae when Mom folds the napkin in front of her. "We need to talk about the lying about QuizBowl."

I knew a consequence was in the works. I suspect this sundae is here to help cushion whatever

I have coming. I brace myself for my sentencing. "Sure," I say.

Mom looks right at me. "Accompany me to the nursery. I want to find some fall flowers to put on the front porch. Then you can come home and help me with some yard work. There are lots of leaves to rake."

Manual labor is how I will be making it up to Mom. After how sick I felt for lying for all these weeks about QuizBowl, it almost feels like not enough.

"Okay," I say. "Is there anything else?"

Mom pushes the bowl to me so I can have the last bite of ice cream. "Yes," she says. "Go back to art club. We've paid for the entire year. You can switch sections, but you need this creative balance in your life."

I sit up. "I'll have to drop another club."

Mom nods. "I know you'll figure it out."

"Mom," I say, "this really isn't that big of a punishment. I'm assigned yard work and need to stick with art club. I can't believe I'm saying this, but I think it should be something more."

Mom stands up and kisses me on my forehead.

"You're rebelling against authority and the social pressure of society. Look at you. Doing things your own way." She smiles. "You're a Miller after all."

I sit back in my chair as the realization comes. With my interest in more intellectual pursuits, I always thought I was different from my carefree family. They do their own thing. Turns out, I am the same. I'm equally opinionated and stubborn. All this time, I thought Mom wanted me to be like her. Turns out, I already am. We are like branches, each forming our own path and destination, but at the same time part of the same family tree.

We spend a few more minutes talking, and then I head to bed. This time I don't care if the only clean pajamas are hot pink, with a pattern of dancing elves.

16.

Sitting in front of me on the table is a lump of clay. The shape gives me no vision of what it could be. The color is a dull mixture of brown and gray that screams boring. From the top of this wet blob of clay to the slick and sticky bottom, I find nothing inspiring about this material.

I lean over to Ryan. She seems deep in thought as she studies the mound in front of her. "This is art?" I whisper. "It's kind of ugly."

Ryan gives me the side eye. "It's not about what you see right now," she says. "Sculpting is about discovering what's underneath."

I pick up the clay. "Nope. I didn't see anything there before, and I don't see it now."

Ryan laughs. "Glad to see you making jokes, Leah."

Her smiles are contagious, and I manage one of my own. After all the stress and secrets of QuizBowl, my parents and I were able to come to a new course of action for my after-school schedule. I would drop chess club on Mondays and switch to the sculpture section of art club.

The ever-loyal friend who also enjoys all things creative, Ryan decided to enroll in this art section with me. Right now, looking at this brown lump of goo, I wonder if I should have fought harder about keeping chess club.

"Don't just poke at it," Ryan says. "You need to really *feel* it. Get your hands dirty. Your intuition will guide you."

I eye the mound on the table. "How is this supposed to give me direction?"

Ryan rolls up her sleeves and squeezes the wet clay in her hands. It squishes out between her fingers and falls on the table. She looks thrilled.

"Pick it up already and just start," she says. "It will come."

"Are you sure there aren't more supplies for us to use?" I ask her. I feel exposed without a pencil box filled with materials to use for this project.

The teacher told us that today all we would need is our hands—we won't be doing any finer detail that will require tools—but I am skeptical. I like the security of an art kit. It's why I like school supplies. All the different pencils, pens, and erasers help me feel organized. Plus, they are so cute. With only my hands and this clay, I feel unarmed without the other materials.

Ryan notices my worried look. She holds out her hands. "This is all you need. Don't think too hard about this. Art is about the feel. Trust your gut."

I lean on my elbows. "What if my gut is telling me I'm in the wrong club and have made a horrible mistake?"

Ryan wipes a clay finger on my arm, leaving a brown streak. "We're in a club. Not a class. There's no grade, and that feeling isn't coming from your gut. It's your overachieving and active brain. Tell it to chill and take a break for the next hour." She points to her chest. "Let your heart take over."

I hold back a giggle. "You are ridiculous."

Ryan pretends to be offended. "No, that would be you. Afraid of making coil pots. This is so easy—a kindergartner can do this."

She's right. The assignment is to make a pot or vase by rolling sections of clay into ropes or snakes and stacking them together. It feels more functional than creative to me, but I'm here to try it. How difficult will it be to roll out clay and make a pot?

I clap my hands together. "All right," I say, trying to work myself up. "Let's do this."

I scoop the ball up and feel the weight.

I pinch off a piece of clay and roll it between my fingers. The clay is wet and sticky. I roll it on the table. As I apply pressure, it becomes a long coil. I do this a few more times so I have a collection of clay ropes. Some are shorter and thinner than others. I figure this will be okay. It's good to have a variety of sizes.

I can picture what my clay pot will look like.

Tallish sides, made out of this muted-color clay. After it dries, I'll get to paint it. Maybe I'll do an ombre effect, where the paint goes from a lighter shade to a darker one. I'm so pleased with my design that I wonder if I've been a sculpture artist all along.

As we mindlessly make coils of clay, Ryan and I chat. It's nice to do something with my hands while my mind wanders along with the conversation. I don't mean to, but I look over at what Ryan's constructing. She's already started to shape her pot.

The bottom of her sculpture looks like a cinnamon roll swirl. The coils go up the sides, with pieces uniform in size and thickness. As she constructs the sides, I watch Ryan dip her fingers in water. This helps to smooth the clay down and glue the coils together.

I try to copy her, but my fingers are too wet. When I form my coils together, they look lopsided and goopy. My sides aren't strong either. I have to keep repairing my ropes because some of them are skinnier. They keep breaking and collapsing into one another.

Regardless, I keep going. I've learned to lower my expectations. I know I'm not going to master something on the first or even fifth try. The same goes for this clay pot. My goal is to finish, no matter the final outcome.

At the end of the session, a pot is sitting in front of me. It isn't as tall as I hoped for, but there is something there. It has an unintentional wave to it, which could be considered a failure if I were going for a symmetrical pot. Or, if I tilt my head and look at it from a different perspective, my pot looks a little more abstract.

We all walk around the room, looking at one another's creations. When I see Ben in the back of the room, I wave. "Hi," I say, tucking my hair back behind my ears. I forget that I still have clay on my fingers, and now it's in my hair.

I pretend that I don't notice and keep talking to Ben. "How long have you been in this sculpture club?" I ask.

"Since the start of school," he says.

Ben's pot is really good. He's made it wider, almost like a bowl. He looks equally surprised to see me. "I go to this and to art club with Mr.

Jeffers on Tuesdays. I heard you dropped out of that one."

I'm still admiring his pot. "Yeah," I say. "I needed to switch. I had another club at the same time. But I'm glad to be in this one."

"QuizBowl?" Ben says. "You did really great."

"Yeah, it was going really well," I say. "Right up until we lost." I point a finger at myself. "Because of me."

Ben shakes his head. "Just like a true leader. Always taking the credit."

I laugh. "You found me out."

"I was really impressed by the team," Ben says. "You all seemed like you were having a lot of fun in the end."

This observation feels almost as good as winning. Besides being the best team, I wanted to learn how to be a good captain. Someone who could bring out the good in others and create a place we belonged. "Thanks, Ben," I say. "You know, if you're ever interested, we could always use alternate players. We only have one sub, and it could be helpful to have another. You know, if you want a break from two art clubs."

Ben brightens. "Really? I'll think about it."

I try to remain cool. "Yeah! It would be great to have you. We also meet at FroGo Café. Sometimes my brother gives us the frozen yogurt hookup."

"As long as the cardinal stays away from me, I think that could work," Ben says with a smile. "I'm not looking to get into a fight with the school mascot anytime soon."

"Don't worry about me," I say with a smile. "I know how to take that bird down."

We talk for a few more minutes, and when we are done, I practically float back to my seat. I'm in QuizBowl. The youngest team captain ever at Kagan Middle. We aren't exactly on an undefeated run, but there's always room for improvement.

I'm also doing something creative right now. Truthfully, making these pots isn't bad. I may actually like it. Izzy and I are better, and the rest of Team Awkward is a great support. I've made friends through QuizBowl and art, and things are going really well.

There may be truth in some of the things

Mom was telling me about losing. Sometimes those failures push us toward the path we needed to be on all along.

Even with the setbacks, it seems like I am a winner after all.

Acknowledgments

Sometimes a friend comes along and shares an idea for a hidden space that only four adorable girls can see. For me, this friend is Joy McCullough. It's been a blast to collaborate on our project and have it become a reality (complete with a secret locker room). I loved how Joy brought Jojo's story to life in book one, and I've adored writing Leah's perspective in book two.

Much gratitude to Aladdin and Simon Kids for jump-starting this series. It's been a pleasure to work with our wonderful editors, Jessica Smith and Anna Parsons. I may have gone to middle school but have forgotten how to put together a schedule. All appreciation to a wonderfully thorough proofreader, Valerie Shea; Karen Sherman, our careful copyeditor, who helped me unravel a confusing timeline; Art Morgan, managing editor; and Karin Paprocki and Mike Rosamilia, designers. Thank you to Laura Catrinella, for giving the girls such personality and spark with the most charming book covers.

ACKNOWLEDGMENTS

We are grateful for the support from Dystel, Goderich, and Bourret, where my agent, Ann Leslie Tuttle, and Joy's agent, Jim McCarthy, both work. They are a formidable team, and it means the world to have them in our corner.

Yamile Saied Méndez is a friend whose generosity I can never adequately repay. Thank you for connecting Joy and me.

I may have never been punched in the face by a mascot, but I know someone who has. Thank you to Selah for letting me borrow this embarrassing moment for Leah's story. Lastly, much love to the Awesome Bybees.